BEYOND
THE SEA OF
DREAMS

MARY ANN SHORT

authorHOUSE®

AuthorHouse™
1663 Liberty Drive
Bloomington, IN 47403
www.authorhouse.com
Phone: 833-262-8899

Published by AuthorHouse 06/22/2021

ISBN: 978-1-6655-2901-3 (sc)
ISBN: 978-1-6655-2899-3 (hc)
ISBN: 978-1-6655-2900-6 (e)

Library of Congress Control Number: 2021911950

Print information available on the last page.

Any people depicted in stock imagery provided by Getty Images are models, and such images are being used for illustrative purposes only. Certain stock imagery © Getty Images.

This book is printed on acid-free paper.

Because of the dynamic nature of the Internet, any web addresses or links contained in this book may have changed since publication and may no longer be valid. The views expressed in this work are solely those of the author and do not necessarily reflect the views of the publisher, and the publisher hereby disclaims any responsibility for them.

This is a work of fiction. All of the characters, names, incidents, organizations, and dialogue in this novel are either the products of the author's imagination or are used fictitiously.

Contents

With love and gratitude to all who have inspired
and supported me in this journey!

Chapter One

"Dad, please I have to go to school. I'll be late for school again!" 18-year-old Dierdre cried.

"Now come over here, Dierdre, and spend some time with me. Hurry up girl! Your mother will be back soon and you know I don't like it when Mother comes home. Now come here and sit with me." He motioned to the sofa.

Dierdre could smell the stale odor of liquor on her father's breath from halfway across the room. She hated when he drank. Alcohol turned her otherwise mild-mannered and even-tempered father into such a monster. The drug changed him from Dr. Jekyll into Mr. Hyde. She hated the way he touched her, the way his hand brushed her upper thigh or developing breasts, almost as if by accident, but clearly intentional. Most frightening was that these advances, which only happened when they were alone in the house, were becoming more frequent. He often walked in on her while showering or dressing. Sometimes, at night, Dierdre could feel his eyes staring at her through the darkened hallway as she slept.

She couldn't help remembering the years when her father, Daniel Farrell, a professor of sociology, was quickly becoming an established and highly respected scholar. He was tall, lean and handsome, and so very intelligent. He may very well have been a genius. Over the years, his consumption of alcohol steadily increased. No one seemed to notice at first, but as his addiction progressed, both physical and emotional changes became apparent. Dierdre couldn't help feeling sorry for him. Still, his behavior and his treatment of her during these periods of drunkenness were growing more intolerable with each passing day.

She breathed a sigh of relief as she heard the back door suddenly open. Mother was home. Now aware of his wife's return, Mr. Farrell mumbled some minor vulgarities under his breath and stepped into his study.

Her mother called out from the kitchen, "Dierdre, what are you still doing home? You're late for school. Honestly, girl, I don't need the attendance officer bothering me again because of your tardiness. Now get going!"

As usual, before Dierdre could get a word in edgewise, her mother had already hastily brushed her off. Dierdre tried on several occasions to discuss her father's drinking problem with her mother, but Louise Farrell was in total denial. That her mother could completely disregard her own husband's state of drunkenness Dierdre just couldn't comprehend.

The professor never drank himself into a stupor in public. At least not yet. To the outside world, he was a true intellectual and respectable professional. He never embarrassed his wife or his children. How long her father could control his public behavior, however, was yet another question. Sooner or later his loss of control would spill into his public and professional life as well. Hopefully, she wouldn't be around much longer to witness his inevitable deterioration and ultimate collapse. Dierdre was a legal adult now, and with that, freedom was calling.

As if dealing with her father's illness wasn't bad enough, Dierdre's relationship with, and sense of belonging to, the family Farrell was virtually nonexistent. She never could understand how her mother, a spoiled young woman from an affluent family on the East Coast, came to marry a relatively poor boy from the Midwest. True, Daniel Farrell was highly intelligent and quite good-looking in his youth. Clearly though, his chosen profession as an educator could not provide the manner of living to which his wife had been accustomed.

Her parents must surely have married out of necessity rather than choice. In 1953, Louise Cunningham and Daniel Farrell were wed and very shortly thereafter her sister Daryia was born. Now a twenty-year-old sophomore attending Florida State College, Daryia was surely her parent's favorite. Besides the fact that she was absolutely gorgeous, a former high school cheerleader, and homecoming queen, she also had a way of getting anything she wanted from practically anyone and everyone, including her parents. Very simply, Daryia was a spoiled brat. She always was. She always would be. Indeed, she was a carbon copy of her mother in every way. If snobbery was a genetic trait, Daryia certainly inherited that gene from the master. The only reason that her sister attended college at all was to snag herself an eligible and handsome potential doctor or lawyer who hailed from good and wealthy stock.

Far from a "straight A" student, Daryia was forced to withdraw from four classes during her first two years of school to keep from flunking out altogether. Yet, despite her limited academic abilities, she seemed to hold the world in the palm of her hand. Regardless of her sister's less than sincere efforts to become an educated and useful member of society, their parents continued to pay not only for her college expenses but also for her very affluent lifestyle. Daryia certainly knew how to get the best out of life with virtually no self-sacrifice.

How the Farrell's afforded Daryia's lavish existence remained a mystery. Her mother hadn't worked in years, and a professor's salary surely couldn't stretch quite so far. Likely the Cunninghams (her grandparents) were serving as the family's money source, although they certainly never showered any of their riches on her.

Dierdre felt like a stranger in her own family, so much so that during her grade school years she believed that she might have been a foster child or that she may have been adopted. Everyone else in the family was so very attractive, well-mannered, and socially sophisticated by nature, while Dierdre was relatively homely in appearance and very much the loner. There was a time when she even thought that the hospital must have mixed up the babies, and that she really belonged to a different family. Indeed, as the years passed, Dierdre came to acknowledge that she was, most definitely, the unwanted child. Her mother searched for any opportunity to inform her that she wished she had never been born. That her mother cursed her from the moment of conception was a difficult and unexplained burden for Dierdre to carry. Why did her own mother dislike her so much?

The only one who truly loved her was the family dog, Max. He was fourteen years old, and getting slower and sicklier with each passing day. The thought of his imminent passing saddened Dierdre. Her heart sank just thinking about it. She marveled at how, despite his pain and discomfort, he forced his arthritic legs to greet her at the door when she came home from school each day. His once thick, shiny, black retriever's coat was now thinned, dulled, and grayed. His once bright, clear eyes now cloudy, and his cool, sweet breath now hot and foul-smelling with age. Yet, Dierdre loved him dearly. She hated to see him suffering and would miss him terribly when he was gone. Could God be so cruel? Could he punish this poor animal with so much discomfort and pain simply because he loved the family outcast? Somehow it didn't seem fair. Then again, nothing in this life was. With that thought she kissed the top of Max's drowsy head and left for school.

Chapter Two

If Dierdre was a stranger to her own family, she certainly had no better sense of belonging with her peers. She held a part-time job as a grocery cashier that left little time for socializing or participating in extracurricular activities. While her fellow high school seniors had no great dislike of her, they clearly expressed no particular interest in her either. Her classmates spent most of their time participating in clubs, dating and partying. Dierdre concentrated her efforts on studying and working. She had little in common with girls her own age. Circumstances at home forced her to think and act more like an adult than a teenager. She was, by all accounts, very mature for an eighteen-year-old, but she liked it that way.

Academics came easily to her. A fast learner with a superior memory, she didn't have to study much. She guessed she inherited her scholastic abilities from her father, who was surely gifted. God probably had to offer her something of value to the real world, so He gave her a good mind. After all, that was the least He could do for her since He gave absolutely everything else to Daryia. Literature and writing classes were her favorites. Although her grades were just as good in math and science, Dierdre preferred to study the fictional worlds created by the masters. She also enjoyed composing her own stories and works of poetry. The literary world was, in many ways, her haven. Dierdre could be anyone she chose to be in an imaginary world. She could dream of a different life there, of a life where she could feel safe, secure, and happy. She could find freedom from the fear and despair of the real world. In her imagination, she could be the most important person in the world, when in real life she was virtually nobody.

At 10 p.m., Dierdre returned home, weak from fatigue. The store was particularly busy on Friday nights since the summer was fast approaching and weekend barbecues and picnics were becoming popular activities for normal families. Good old Max greeted her at the door, as always. He knew her schedule well by now. He would begin the painful journey from his favorite spot alongside the fireplace long before her arrival. His walk halfway across the house must have seemed like a marathon, but he never failed her. She bent to rub his oversized ears. Along with life's certainties of death and taxes stood dearest Max, as dependable as ever.

Her parents were in the den. Her father was passed out on the sofa in his usual drunken state and her mom gossiped on the telephone with one of her nosy and stuck-up friends. In this last week of May, Dan Farrell's teaching semester had ended two weeks earlier. He drank the entire day away. He often did so when not working. Maybe he would be offered a few classes for the summer session that began in June. Part-time work for the summer would keep him sober at least some of the time. Dierdre reckoned that he must be a very sad and lonely man to have chosen a path that led only to self-destruction. How could this be happening to him? How could her mother allow him to do this to himself, to all of them?

Wearily, Dierdre headed up the stairs that led to her bedroom. Her mother, still deeply engrossed in her criticisms of some poor soul that was selected for the evening's chopping block of gossip, didn't blink an eye to acknowledge her presence.

Dierdre left Max at the foot of the stairs, his legs having lost the strength to follow her up long ago.

"Good night, Max. See you tomorrow," she called from the top of the staircase, as he lifted his heavy, but still loving eyes, in acknowledgment.

Dierdre methodically changed into her nightclothes, brushed her hair and teeth, and pulled down the bed covers. For a brief moment, she considered doing some homework. No, too tired. She tucked herself under the comforter and switched off the lights.

A multitude of thoughts raced through her mind. Only a few short weeks were left to the end of another school year. The annual senior trip was on the calendar of upcoming events. As usual, Dierdre wouldn't be going. The class yearbook was published and available for purchase. She wouldn't be buying one. The guidance counselors were scheduling meetings with students to finalize college admissions. She didn't bother to make an appointment. Dierdre didn't want to know about any of these things. All she wanted was for the school year to be completed.

Coming of age meant more than existence. It meant life. Freedom to leave this house and the people in it. To find a place in the world where she really belonged. A place where her thoughts and feelings mattered. With a heavy but hopeful heart, she fell off to sleep and dreamed of all of the possibilities.

Chapter Three

Time dragged on as the end of the school year approached. Dierdre decided to take advantage of the impending summer vacation and, without a moment's hesitation, committed to more hours at the market. On the whole, she enjoyed working. Her supervisors at the grocery, as well as the customers, seemed to like her, and the money wasn't bad.

Her father would soon be teaching two classes per week. Although his drinking remained heavy, at least it didn't appear to have worsened. In addition, the Farrell's social calendar was filled with a number of summer events that her mother had planned. All of these activities would help to temporarily relieve Dierdre of some of the pressures of recent months regarding her father's behavior. She was rarely alone in the house with him now, and that was good.

Word came that Daryia would be home from college before weeks end. No great love existed between them. Daryia became the center of attention whenever she came home. Dierdre couldn't help being amused by the show. The coming months would be like a feature-length film straight out of Hollywood. Daryia was, of course, "the star," her parents acting in "supporting roles," and Dierdre, a "bit part extra." How good a performance would they all put in this year? Who knew? Who cared? Dierdre was an adult now. Soon she would graduate and be free of them.

Once she left she might never return. Some days dawned when she couldn't help conceding to her fears and anxieties in that regard. Yet, the thought of her life continuing as it was left her afraid and anxious too. Dierdre wanted desperately to be somebody, to be free to express herself, but no room existed for her personal self-expression in the Farrell household. Recognizing the difficulty in trying to create oneself in an atmosphere of indifference, Dierdre's frustration only grew with the passage of time. So much occurred that she didn't understand, but what did it matter? After all, she was just a "bit part extra."

Louise Farrell planned a huge welcome home dinner for Daryia who was scheduled to arrive on the last Friday in May. Daniel managed to be relatively sober to mark the occasion. Dierdre had almost forgotten what he was like when sober. He looked about ten years younger when he wasn't drinking. Why was everyone so happy to see Daryia? After all, she never brought home a respectable report card, nor even began to pretend she was happy to be home. A visit home for Daryia was clearly like a visit to the bank. She stayed just long enough to transact a withdrawal of funds to support the next few months of her always on-the-run lifestyle, only to return again when the well ran dry. Of the three to four months of free time between semesters last year, Daryia spent only three weeks of it at the family home. The rest of the time she traveled about with her college friends (most of them men, since other young women found competing with her well-rehearsed charm difficult) and spent an awful lot of somebody else's money. Whatever the case, Daryia was on her way home and, if Dierdre was lucky, everyone would be so obsessed with her sister's presence that they would leave her alone. That would suit her just fine. The less involvement and interaction with this excuse for a family the better.

Daryia arrived at the family house over three hours later than expected. Dinner was ruined as a result, and typically, Daryia showed little concern for everyone's inconvenience. Despite her unexplained tardiness, she was greeted with great fanfare by her parents and grandparents alike. Dierdre thought she would barf. As much as Dierdre hated to admit it, she couldn't deny that her sister looked fabulous. To say that she was "pretty" didn't do justice to her naturally beautiful face and perfect figure. Daryia held a striking resemblance to her mother.

They had very similar facial features, and even their hair and body types were comparable. The most distinctive of her sister's features, however, were her deep green eyes. No one else in the family had them and they were mesmerizing.

Dinner was eventually served and Dierdre was obliged to listen to hours of boring conversation. She was grateful when the evening finally came to an end and she could retreat to the solace of her own room. In bed, she listened to the chattering of her mother and sister from across the hallway. Both incredibly social and exceptionally beautiful, they were like caviar or fine wine. As she closed her eyes searching for sleep, all Dierdre could wonder was why she felt like chopped liver.

Chapter Four

Weeks passed and little changed. Daniel drank excessively, and his wife seemed less concerned than ever about anything but her own social agenda, which included her husband less and less. Max was still hanging on, bless him, despite being totally deaf and almost blind. As Dierdre neared the end of her senior year, Max stopped greeting her at the door. She guessed he could barely muster up the strength to lift his head to eat and could hardly walk at all. He would likely pass on before she graduated, but it was just as well. She was already making plans to graduate in June and then be gone from this unhappy place. She could never take Max with her and would surely despair at leaving him behind in a home that knew every four letter word in the dictionary except "love."

Dierdre wasn't going to the senior prom. She never had a boyfriend in high school so the thought of attending never even crossed her mind. The prom was, however, all the other girls could talk about for weeks. They gossiped about who was going, who wasn't going, what everyone was wearing, and what cars they would be driving. They also talked about being toasted on booze, high on weed, and having sex in the back of a limousine. Dierdre supposed she was the only virgin in town, or maybe in the state, or even the world. She wondered how many girls would get pregnant on prom night. How many girls had already had abortions? How anyone could enjoy having their private parts invaded by strange and drunken hands? She so hated when her father tried to touch her. The smell of his sour breath alone was enough to make her sick, but to allow a man the privilege of knowing her – – no way! Her body and soul were the only God-given things that were truly hers alone. No one would have their way with either.

In a few short weeks Dierdre would be free of her parent's selfish indifference. They knew nothing of her plans to leave, and she was determined that nothing they could say or do would change her mind even if they found out. She wouldn't let them talk her into staying, no matter what, although likely they wouldn't care enough to even try.

Dierdre managed to save almost three thousand dollars from years of hard work at the grocery store. Although not a lot of money by any means, it was enough to make a fresh start. She had no current plans to attend college and that truly saddened her. Her parents offered neither emotional nor financial support regarding a college education. Daryia was likely bleeding them dry financially and her father's becoming so ill didn't help the situation. Again, just as well. She didn't want to owe anyone anything. All she wanted was a new and different life. Soon, she would begin a new position as a proofreader for a publishing company in the city. Although only an entry-level position, with minimum pay, it was a start. A new beginning.

Dierdre loved the city atmosphere. So much excitement and opportunity pulsated everywhere. This change was to mark the start of a life that, to date, had stood frozen in time. Soon she would be searching for an apartment of her own in a place far away. As each day passed, Dierdre smiled at the thought of it. Only a few more weeks to freedom. She couldn't wait.

Graduation day came quickly and all of her classmates were anxiously running about the school gymnasium waving to their families and friends seated in the bleachers. Dierdre felt awkward in her blue and gold cap and gown, somewhat like a clown in the circus. How she hated spectacles! Soon the band would play pomp and circumstance and the graduates of the class of 1975 would begin their procession amidst the loving and adoring eyes of their family and friends. Numerous parties would progress throughout the evening and the weekend; house parties, beach parties, open parties and private parties.

As she and her classmates proceeded to the podium to receive their diplomas, enormous relief welled within her. When her turn came to receive her certificate, she shook the principal's hand and waved to her absentee family in the grandstands just as her classmates did. The Farrell house would host no party for Dierdre, and typically, she had not been invited to anyone else's. Yet, soon the gates of her emotional prison would be unlocked and, like a caged bird, she would fly through that open door to freedom. The world would now be hers for the taking. Well, part of it anyway, and any part, no matter how small, was better than what she had obtained to date, which was virtually nothing at all. Nothing good. Nothing bad. Just nothing.

Max died in his sleep two days after Dierdre's graduation. She discovered him curled up in his usual place. She called to him, but he didn't lift his head or blink his eyes. A sick feeling grew in her stomach with each step towards him. She could feel that his body was still warm, but the breath of life was gone from him. She fought hard not to cry, but found it impossible to control the flood of tears that fell down her face. She wrapped her arms around Max's lifeless body and held him close to her heart. Now, she was truly alone. The only emotional connection to her family was severed. Her only friend in the world had passed on to another time and place. A part of her was angry with God for taking him away, while yet another part wished she could have gone with him.

As Max began to grow cold and stiff, she composed herself, said one final prayer for his soul, and then dragged him to a wooded area behind the house where she dug the large hole and laid his heavy, rigid body to rest. She received no assistance or sympathy from her parents. Her mother exclaimed relief at "getting that smelly old dog out of the house," and her father, typically, removed himself from the situation with a bottle of booze.

Dan Farrell's drinking had become even more excessive in the past month. On several occasions, he was too drunk to lecture and his department chair sent him home rather than chance the embarrassment. Had it not been for so many years of tenured service with the college, he would surely have been fired, but worse, his behavior at home had become almost impossible to control. He stared at Dierdre constantly, his eyes red and glazed, and spoke words under his breath that she couldn't understand. Her mother was rarely home. Dierdre thought that she might be having an affair. Her father, she was certain, knew something she didn't, and whatever he knew, it was driving him crazy.

In just another ten days Dierdre would be gone. She wondered if she would ever see her father again. If the alcohol didn't kill him, depression surely would, but she steeled herself against compassion. She had enough problems of her own, most of which would be remedied with her imminent departure.

Chapter Five

The quiet of the late evening was unsettling. Dierdre was exhausted from packing suitcases and wading through eighteen-years of accumulated junk. She was leaving in two days and, perhaps, anticipation and anxiety were largely responsible for her weary state. She was taking mostly clothing and incidentals to a small, sparsely furnished apartment in the city that would be available on the first of July. It was far from a class act, but affordable, and in a relatively decent and safe part of town. Everything was moving so fast now. Although drained from the sudden rush of activity in her life in the past month, the anticipation kept her awake for the past several nights. Who could blame her? In one more day she would be on her way to beginning a new and hopefully better life. With that in mind, Dierdre turned onto her side and counted sheep into a deep and peaceful slumber.

Her sleep was heavy and dreamless until a light in the hallway abruptly awakened her. She looked at the alarm clock. 2 a.m. No sound came from the corridor and she quickly covered her head with a pillow. She assumed her father was drinking again. He often wandered through the house at night. Sometimes she could even hear his heavy breathing behind her door, but he didn't linger in the hallway that night. Rather, his footsteps were unusually swift and purposeful. She didn't hear the toilet, nor movement up or down the stairway. What in heaven's name was he doing out there? God, sometimes he made her so nervous, she thought, struggling to get back to sleep.

Dierdre awoke with a stale, dry taste in her mouth and lazily turned again towards the clock. Almost noon. Still half asleep, she wandered into the bathroom. The house was very still. Her mother spent Saturday mornings at the beauty salon and her father was most likely still asleep. The booze made him sleep nearly all day. She reckoned he was either awake and drunk or asleep and drunk. Sobriety was a virtually nonexistent state for Dan Farrell at this stage of the game.

Her shower felt more invigorating than usual. Dierdre carefully wrapped her freshly washed hair into a small, absorbent towel, draped herself in a white, terrycloth robe and proceeded back to her room. The stench of alcoholic breath grew stronger with each step she took. Through the half-open bedroom door, she could see him sitting on the edge of her bed with his hands folded in his lap. He looked up, half-dazed, as she entered. His now deeply lined face was drawn and pinched, and his expression vacant.

"Daddy, go back to bed!" she scolded as if he were a child. "You've had too much to drink!"

He laughed quietly to himself, staring at the floor. "Daddy doesn't want to sleep. Daddy wants his little girl."

"Dad, please," Dierdre insisted, "please leave me alone. I have a lot to do today and I have to get dressed. Please just leave my room. Leave me alone!"

His narrowed eyes grew fiery, and despite his significantly alcohol-impaired coordination, he reached for her arm swiftly and unexpectedly.

"Don't you tell me what to do!" He screamed, lunging towards her. "Everyone is always telling me what to do, what to say, what to give, what to take! I will take what I damn please!"

"Dad, please, please! Please go! Can't you see that you need help?"

"Help, oh yes, I need help! Why then don't you help me?" He asked as he reached for the tie to robe.

Swiftly he attacked. Dierdre shrieked as he struck her with the back of his fist. She couldn't remember how many times she felt his teeth bite into her tender, naked flesh. He was all over her. His rough and cold hands invaded every part of her body, and his slobbering mouth dribbled slime. She was going to be sick. She tried desperately to break free of him, but wasn't strong enough to fight him off. Surely she was still asleep and having a nightmare. This couldn't be real.

Oh my God! Her mind cried out. Oh my God this can't be happening! Somebody stop him! Please, God, make him stop! Please, God! Please! I'm leaving tomorrow. Just one more day until tomorrow! Her heart wept, but no one heard.

He quickly fled from the room when he was done. Dierdre sat, naked and cross-legged beside her bed in a state of shock. She could feel the rush of tears from her eyes and could hear herself whimpering. She tried to convince herself that such a horrible thing could not have just happened to her.

"This is not real, not real!" She insisted as she threw her red and swollen face into her hands and wept.

Several hours passed before Dierdre could bring herself to some reasonable state of composure. How she hated her father and her entire family! All of them lived only to take, as though to give were a mortal sin. Perhaps in the devil's company, it was. Today, her father had taken from her not only her innocence, but also what little remained of her dignity and self-respect. She'd been beaten and abused, and everyone, not just Daniel Farrell, was to blame. Her mother allowed her husband to drink himself into madness, and by cursing the day Dierdre was born, disabled her self-esteem. Her grandparents treated her like a stray dog for as long as she could remember. Her sister was blatant in her expression of abhorrence and embarrassment towards Dierdre, and her schoolmates were obvious in their indifference. And what about God? Where was He when the feelings of self-doubt and self-hate that plagued Dierdre for all eighteen years of her life had taken her to this horrible place? Where was His mercy and love now?

Filled with fear and confusion, she still knew that she had no choice but to pull herself together so that she could get out of the house as quickly as possible. Sleeping on a park bench would be safer than sleeping in the family home for one more night. Leaving, immediately, was the only answer. Her mother would be home soon. No way existed to explain what had just happened. Her father would never admit to what he had done, and more than likely wouldn't even remember, and her mother would surely say that she was lying, or worse...

She peaked beyond the still half-open doorway. The corridor was clear. Her father was likely somewhere in the house, but if she were lucky, he was passed out and would remain so for several more hours. Frantically, she threw on her Levi's, sweatshirt, and sneakers, and tossed whatever remained of her personal belongings into her suitcases. She worried that she might be forgetting something of importance, but for the moment, just getting out of the house was top priority. She wished she could take another shower to wash the violation from her body, but there was no time for that now. She had to get downstairs to call a taxi. She would ask to be picked up at the next street over, and thus avoid any confrontation with her mother, who was already overdue. Quickly, she glanced once more around her room and realized that no fond memories remained to be left behind here. Purposeful and determined, bags in hand, she ran out of the room and down the staircase as if caught by a whirlwind. Still no sign of her father. Good. She reached desperately for the telephone on the kitchen wall.

"I need a cab, right away!" She pleaded with a woman on the other end, as she proceeded to babble the address of a residence on the next block.

"Ten minutes, ma'am," the woman said, and hung up immediately. Ten minutes.

Dierdre scrambled with her belongings that weighed heavily on her bruised and weary arms. Scampering, half-crazed, out the back door she headed down the street and around the corner to wait. Five minutes went by. Then ten.

"Oh, God, where is this guy?" She cried. "Hurry, please hurry!"

While she was waiting, she suddenly realized that she had nowhere to go since her apartment would not be available until Monday morning.

"Damn!" She said aloud. "Oh, what the hell," she said. "I'll spring for a hotel for the night. After all, I should be celebrating. This is the day Dierdre Farrell becomes a free and independent woman at last."

Shamed crucifixion behind her, her resurrection was at hand.

Almost concurrently with that thought, the taxi arrived. The driver loaded her bags and asked, "Where to?"

Securely in the backseat she answered, "The city, please."

"Are you crazy? You got the money for that? Not that I like to turn away business, but it's a lot cheaper to take the bus," he said.

"No, I'm not crazy," she answered. "Yes, I have the money and there is no time for a bus. Please, let's go now!"

"It's your money," he said.

As the driver shifted the transmission into drive and pulled away from the curb, Dierdre let out a huge sigh of relief. The driver chose a route out of the housing development that passed directly in front of her home. With a large lump in her throat, Dierdre watched as her mother's car pulled into their driveway. She ducked as the cab cruised right in front of the house and stayed low in the backseat for at least two miles thereafter. When she finally had the courage to sit up, she looked out the rear window and prayed no one had seen or followed her. No one did. She was free. Praise God, she was finally free.

Chapter Six

At 6 p.m., the taxi entered onto the freeway. The traffic heading west was relatively light. Another hour or so would pass before they would reach the city. Breathing a deep sigh of relief, Dierdre had time to sort out her thoughts and feelings. As she watched the trees pass with swiftness along the roadside, she wondered what her parents would think when they realized that she was gone and had left no forwarding address or phone. Likely, her mother would be too self-absorbed to notice, and her father would, surely, be relieved that his incestuous crime, even if he did remember it, would remain a well-guarded secret. Dierdre cringed. Her skin crawled with feelings of uncleanliness, but she had to be strong. Having all else stripped from her, her sanity was all she had left. She had to at least hold onto that. No one would ever violate her again. No one would take from her without asking. No one would get close enough to hurt her. She had lived her entire life without friends or loving family and after this day, what greater horror could befall her? Dierdre could never begin to comprehend why God had sealed for her such a lonely and tear-filled fate, but she was determined to be a survivor.

Throbs of pain pulsed from the bruised parts of her body. Her right eye felt swollen. She wasn't sure if it was from crying or from being beaten. She hoped it didn't look as puffy as it felt. Every part of her body ached. Her legs felt heavy and chafing of relatively tight jeans against her groin (sore from her father's forceful violation) made it difficult to sit in any one position for any length of time. She tried desperately to put the day's events out of her conscious mind, but the physical discomfort only continued to remind her. A hot bath and a good meal would do her well, she determined, as she dozed off to sleep for a spell.

Dierdre awoke to horns blowing and people shouting all around her.

"Where are you staying?" the driver asked.

In her desperation, she hadn't given a thought to where she would stay for the night. She handed him a scrap of paper with the address of her new apartment scribbled on it and answered, "The nearest hotel to here."

The cabbie pulled up to a small, but seemingly respectable hotel about two miles from the address she gave him. "This look okay, Lady?"

"Yes, it looks fine," she said, hoping that the pleasant looking exterior was indicative of the interior as well. "How much do I owe you?"

"That'll be sixty-two dollars."

Dierdre handed him three twenty-dollar bills and a ten. "Thank you, sir, and keep the change."

Abruptly, he stashed the cash in his trouser pocket and began unloading her bags onto the sidewalk. Dierdre got the distinct impression that she would be carrying them into the reception area herself. She wished the driver would have offered to be more helpful, but it seemed his courtesy stopped at the curb. With a toot of the horn and a wave of the hand, the driver pulled away leaving Dierdre standing alone on the corner. Virtually exhausted, she bent over to lift her bags, with weary bones cracking. She struggled with the double doors providing entrance to the lobby, and nearly tripped over her own feet.

"May I have a room, please?" She asked, although the words came out sounding more like a plea.

A pleasant looking, middle-aged woman with white hair and wire rimmed glasses pursed her lips and raised her eyebrows at the sight of her. "Room 302." She handed an elderly bellman the key. "That will be one hundred and twenty dollars for the night."

Reluctantly, Dierdre rummaged through her purse and handed the desk clerk another stack of twenty-dollar bills. She then proceeded to follow the bellman to her room, gracefully offered him a generous tip, and closed the door behind her. Right about now she was so tired that she could fall asleep standing up. Despite growing feelings of hunger (she hadn't eaten since Friday night), all that mattered at the moment was bathing away the morning's assault.

The hotel room was comfortably decorated in color combinations of pink and blue. The small-print flowered wallpaper was pleasing to the eye, and the golden oak furniture was simplistic in its style and character. Low-intensity lighting gave everything in the room a soothing, amber-like glow. Dierdre kicked off her sneakers and lay back on the full-sized bed. How good to rest on the soft, warm mattress. As she pulled a pillow to her chest, she gazed through the sheer draperies and could see the sun beginning to set in the sky. She scanned the room as her body rested on the bed. She caught sight of the door that led to the bath. She hated disturbing the comfort that her dog-tired body needed so desperately, but knew that she couldn't sleep unless cleansed of her father's lust.

Dierdre lifted herself to an upright position and slowly began to undress. Every movement caused her pain, each stretch of an arm or leg, every bend of her head and neck. Clad only in her cotton panties, she accidentally caught a glimpse of her half-naked body in the mirror. Oh, God! Her face was red and swollen and her left cheekbone appeared twice its normal size. She could plainly see the beginnings of black and blue marks on her arms and the bluish-purple remnants of the teeth that savagely bit into the tender flesh of her neck. Sweet Jesus, what must the cabbie, desk clerk, and bellman have thought at the sight of her? Was this reflection in the mirror possibly her own? How she looked on the outside couldn't begin to compare to the way she felt on the inside. She wanted to cry, but fought the tears. Crying wouldn't change anything.

Abruptly, Dierdre turned away from the mirror in disgust, walked into the bath and turned on the faucets to fill the tub. When the tub was three-quarters full, she immersed herself, only to realize that she was still wearing her underwear. Stepping back, she removed her panties, and saw the blood. The evidence of violation was so ugly. With the blood-stained garment still in her hand, Dierdre sat in the tub. She reached for a bar of soap and began to wash the stains from the delicate material. They weren't coming out. Frantically, she scrubbed the panties over and over again, but the stains remained. She soaked and scrubbed until the material was practically torn to shreds, but still she wasn't satisfied that they were clean. She began to cry. She was sobbing so hard that she could barely breathe. In a state of near hysteria, she jumped out of the tub. With her body naked and dripping wet, she scampered to the nearest window, opened it and threw the now tattered garment into the night air as far as she possibly could. Quickly, she shut and locked the window, drew the drapes closed and then stopped to take a series of long, deep breaths. Satisfied and relieved, Dierdre positioned her bruised body once again into the warmth of the tub, and allowed its pure, clean water to melt away the sorrowful memories that she was determined to leave far behind her.

Chapter Seven

Although she awoke to an overcast day and threatening rainstorms, even inclement weather could not put a damper on her peaceful and well-rested mood. Dierdre sat up and her stomach growled. She hadn't eaten in nearly two days and was absolutely famished. Throwing a towel around her naked body, she lazily meandered into the bathroom and took a long look at her face in the mirror. The swelling appeared to have gone down a bit and the dark circles under her hazel eyes seemed less pronounced. With some creative makeup, she might actually be a presentable member of the human race again.

She made a promise to herself that today would mark a new beginning. Now free from the torments of the past, she alone would control her fate. She would discover the real Dierdre Farrell. The Dierdre Farrell whose thoughts and feelings had been so repressed by the uncaring and self-absorbed people who called themselves her family.

Downstairs, the sweet and savory French toast and sausages she ordered for breakfast settled comfortably in her belly. Dierdre scanned the dining room as a gentle rain splashing on the windowsill soothed her. Although the eatery was full, she was the only person sitting alone, but no one seemed to notice her solitary state. In the suburbs, no one dined alone, or went to the movies alone, or to parties alone. Everything in the burbs was geared towards either couples or group activities. Yet, the city seemed different. The people here were more secure as individuals, not needing to hide themselves behind crowds of other people or convenient, but unfeeling friends and lovers. In the city, to live, eat, walk, play, sleep, or die alone, was perfectly acceptable. No shame or embarrassment in independence or uncensored self-expression existed. Yes, Dierdre would adjust easily to this lifestyle. Despite her insecurities, she had always been a loner and believed that survival in this environment would be a challenge to which she looked forward. Besides, what did she have to lose?

When she returned to her room, the rain had trickled down to a soft drizzle. Dierdre donned a light windbreaker from her still unpacked luggage and headed onto the urban streets. The air was thick with humidity, but the light sprinkle of rain against her cheeks felt cool and refreshing. To stretch her legs, and to breathe in some fresh, clean air was therapeutic for both body and mind. On this Sunday morning, the avenues were relatively quiet. With her hands in her pockets and her head held high, Dierdre walked for miles. She strolled through a small tree-lined park and saw the apartment building where she would be dwelling for at least the next year. She spent the rest of the morning and the better part of the afternoon becoming quietly acquainted with the neighborhood. The handfuls of people on the street were pleasant-looking, and although no one stopped to say hello, many reflexively broke into smiles as they passed.

By early afternoon, the hot summer sun was breaking through the passing rain clouds. Dierdre could have sworn that she saw a rainbow on the way back to the hotel. By the time she approached the building, the rain and humidity had entirely burned off and the air, although still hot, was fresh and dry. Her pace quickened as an eerie sense said that someone was following her. She glanced behind her. No one. She continued to walk rapidly, sneaking a peek over her shoulder every couple of yards. Still, no one. Yet, the feeling that someone or something was watching her remained very intense. Was she just being paranoid? She had, after all, been through a great deal in the past two days and the trauma was unsettling.

"It's just my nerves," she said, as she began to walk even more quickly, taking an alternate route to the hotel.

She would feel better when she got inside. Perhaps she was forcing her acceptance and adjustment to this new environment just a bit too much for the first day out. Yes, that's what it is, she told herself.

No one could have known to where she had fled, and if anyone did, they wouldn't care enough to have followed her anyway. Or would they? Dierdre had just about convinced herself that her imagination had been running away with her when she turned the corner towards the back side of the hotel. The landscape looked surprisingly familiar as she realized that the view from her room was on this side of the building. With head tilted upward, she recognized the pink and blue draperies decorating the third-floor window. A sick feeling suddenly ran through every fiber of her flesh and bone. Instantly, she looked down at her feet and there, crumpled in a murky puddle, lay her tattered underpants. They were wet and mud stained. Or were they bloodstained? She didn't want to know. All she wanted was to be as far away from the memories they evoked as possible. Would the curse of her father's violation of her body and soul never stop haunting her? Angrily kicking at the delicate garment that reminded her of all that she despised, and determined to rid her consciousness of the past, her feet shuffled and stuffed the material down the nearest sewer. Satisfied that she was now finally free of all evidence of Daniel Farrell's greatest sin, Dierdre continued around the corner to the hotel entrance. She ran up to her room and wept until the sun went down.

Dierdre awakened to growing darkness. The clock radio on the nightstand blinked well after 8 p.m. Her day of deliverance was now only hours away. She couldn't help noticing the couples clenching at the dinner tables that night. They all looked so in love. Or maybe it wasn't love. Maybe it was just plain lust, sin, or selfish desire. How she despised that look. The boys in school wore that same look painted on their faces twenty-four hours a day. Her father had that identical look every time he drank too much. He had that look on the day he attacked her, the day he robbed her of her innocence. Here and now, all of these couples gazed at each other with the same invading stare. Dierdre envisioned them all getting drunk as skunks and then screwing the night away. That half of these people were married, but perhaps not to each other, wouldn't matter. If they began the night as strangers, by morning they would be well-acquainted.

As she lay in bed that evening, Dierdre overheard the heavy breathing, whining, and whimpering of heated sex through the thin hotel walls. The noise was impossible to ignore, and went on all night long, but she didn't care. Feeling great comfort in her own sobriety, and in her desire to just be left alone, neither wanting, nor needing anyone, was all that mattered now.

Chapter Eight

Early the next day, Dierdre's head was filled with so many thoughts as she hastily gathered what was left of her scattered belongings. A part of her hated her family emphatically, but a part also pitied them. She considered all of the years spent playing second-fiddle to Daryia. She had wished so often that she was more physically attractive and socially popular and yet, Dierdre so despised everything her sister represented. God, she hated her so! And her mother too, a selfish, wicked woman. And then, of course, her father. He was such a sick man. If she pitied anyone, it was him, despite everything he had done to her. Dierdre despised and pitied them all, but now they would play no further part in her life. She felt sure that no one could possibly know to where she had fled and, likely, no one cared. The indifference that tormented her throughout her childhood now brought her the sense of security and emotional freedom for which she had so longed. As Dierdre lifted her suitcases from the floor and out into the hallway, she took one last look at the suite that had been her home for the past two days. It was the most peaceful and comfortable home she had ever known.

The natural beauty of the sunrise absorbed all of her senses. The day was sunny and warm, the kind that makes a person feel good even when she wakes up in a sour mood. Dierdre anxiously paid the balance of her hotel bill to the clerk. Invigorated, she couldn't wait to get to her new apartment. She was scheduled to meet the landlord at 8 a.m. The clock in the lobby read 6:55. The apartment was only a twenty minute walk away, but Dierdre decided to arrive a little early.

She was so excited that she barely felt the weight of her bags as they tugged at her still sore and weary arms. It seemed no time at all before she spotted the brownstone structure standing proud and sturdy amidst the bright morning sun. The building was divided into five separate apartments, three had separate bedrooms and two were studios. Dierdre was renting the smaller of the two studio dwellings. Although financial limitations played a significant role in the available options, she was pleased with her choice just the same. As she waited for the landlord, sitting cross-legged on the front steps, she pictured the studio. Although it was quite small, the layout created a feeling of greater space. Windows on the sides facing both east and west afforded the dwelling a warm and sunny atmosphere for the better part of the day. Dierdre smiled. She couldn't wait to get inside and to begin decorating around the plain furnishings that came with the apartment. She pictured huge floor pillows, five or six of them, spread throughout the living area. A giant floor plant, maybe a philodendron, and a few hanging spider plants in the windows would thrive and help to accentuate the comfortable and casual look she wished to create. The walk-in kitchen area was too small for a table. The long countertop and barstools would simply have to do for dining arrangements. She was lucky to have a full bath. Few studios in the city had a bathtub as well as a shower. Her mind drifted to the chocolate brown-colored curtain covering the shower when she first viewed the place.

"That will have to go," she said aloud, as she was startled by a sudden tap on the shoulder.

A thin, elderly, white-haired gentleman greeted her with a grin. "Nice day to daydream, isn't it? Didn't mean to scare you."

"Oh, hello, Mr. D'Angelo," Dierdre answered, smiling from ear to ear. "It's good to see you again."

"Well, young lady, are you ready to settle in? We are ready for you," he said smiling back at her.

"Oh, yes, I'm ready. Let's go!"

"Let me help you," said the landlord, as he proceeded to carry her bags up the steps.

"Oh, no, please, let me carry them!"

"No, I will help you. You look very tired and you're a nice, young girl. I have three granddaughters just like you. Nice girls, too. We will settle you in."

Why did she deserve such kindness from a stranger? But Dierdre wasn't about to complain. She hadn't been at all anxious about carrying her heavy luggage up any more flights of stairs.

Mr. D'Angelo led them up two flights to apartment number five. As he opened the door, Dierdre could immediately see and feel the warmth of the morning sun coming through the east window.

"Here are your keys," said Mr. D'Angelo, as he pressed them firmly into her hand. "The other renters are very nice here. Across the hall is Marion. She's a young girl, like you. Starting college in the fall. On the second floor is a very lovely couple in apartment number two, John and Lisa Reese. They are new here, too. And Steve Sampson is in apartment three. He's a musician. Between you and me, a little quirky, but he pays the rent. And you know that I live on the first floor. I'll leave you now. The rent is due the first of every month. If you need anything, you call me, okay? I'll see you later."

"Thank you, Mr. D'Angelo. Thank you so much."

"Everybody calls me Mr. D. You call me Mr. D., okay?"

"Sure, thanks, Mr. D. Mrs. D. must be a very lovely person to have such a kind man for a husband, and your children and grandchildren are lucky too," Dierdre said smiling.

"Mrs. D. passed on three years ago," he said, his eyes tearing slightly. "But you're right. She was a very sweet woman and lucky to have married me too."

They laughed.

"See you later, Miss Dierdre."

"See you later, Mr. D."

She waved as he proceeded down the hard and squeaky stairs. Her eyes followed his slow-moving, frail body until it was no longer in sight. He seemed to like her. She liked him too. She took a deep breath and turned sharply back toward the entrance of her apartment.

Not too shabby. With a little work this house would be a home in no time.

She closed the door behind her and rolled up her sleeves. By 5 p.m. that evening the entire apartment was white-glove clean from floor to ceiling. Dierdre unpacked her belongings, had gone shopping for groceries, and even hung a new shower curtain. She looked around the one-room flat and beamed.

Not bad if I say so myself, she thought, walking into her kitchen, to set her table, and to prepare her dinner, in her new home.

Home. What a wonderful word. A word that previously had no meaning to her. Finally, such a place existed in her life, and it was beautiful.

Chapter Nine

Dierdre prepared a light supper of tossed salad, freshly made New England clam chowder from a neighboring fish market, and French bread. She pondered over her meal all that she still had to do to complete her settling in. Soon, she would arrange for a telephone and shop for new clothes for work. She didn't need a car in the city, thank goodness, since she surely couldn't afford one just yet. Generally, things were moving ahead quite smoothly, and although she was still fighting off feelings of anxiety, Dierdre grew stronger in both body and mind with each passing minute. She was determined to move ahead and experience the many joys that life had to offer. A tormented childhood and adolescence would not dampen her spirit. Her time of discovery was at hand. A knock tapped on the door. Who could that be? "God, please don't let anyone have found me," she begged. Afraid to answer, she waited. Silence. Then another knock.

"Hello there. Is anybody home?" A male voice called out from the hallway. Oddly, the strangeness of his voice relieved her.

"Just a minute," she said, as she hurriedly placed the last dirty dish in the sink. Tentatively, she opened the door a crack. "Can I help you?" Several unknown men and women stood in the doorway.

With a smile, the taller of the women displayed a bottle of cheap champagne. "Howdy, neighbor. Welcome to the best apartment house in town. I'm Marion. This is John and his wife Lisa. And oh, that's Steve."

"How nice. You really shouldn't have. Please, come in." Dierdre escorted them into the small living area.

"We couldn't let the day end without saying hello. After all, that would be downright unneighborly," Marion teased in a put-on southern accent.

"Well, I appreciate your neighborliness." Dierdre motioned her guests to make themselves comfortable. "Sorry I haven't any fancy glasses, only the ones that came with the place. I hope you don't mind."

Dierdre took out some very old tumblers from the cupboard, grateful she'd already rinsed off the film and spots that they had apparently worn for quite some time. Either the glasses hadn't been used in ages, or the previous tenant didn't much like to do dishes. Dierdre brought the glasses to her guests as Steve, rather expertly, popped the champagne cork. He took little care to avoid spraying her freshly cleaned living room.

"I'm sorry I haven't any snacks or anything," Dierdre apologized again.

"She sure digs apologizing, doesn't she?" John joked to the others.

"Leave her alone!" Lisa scolded her husband. "We're here to make her feel welcome, not put her on the spot. Just pay my husband no mind. He can be a real pain in the ass. And please don't apologize to us. People who come calling unannounced and uninvited shouldn't expect paper cups and chewing gum, never mind anything else."

They stayed for about two hours and, surprisingly, Dierdre enjoyed their company. By evening's end she had each of their personality types quite comprehensively analyzed in her mind. She spent an awful lot of years on the outside looking in, observing people, their facial expressions, body movements, tone of voice, and the way they sat, walked, talked, looked, and listened. She had come to believe that she was actually very good at sizing up the essence of a person with great accuracy, right down to guessing someone's birth sign. As her new neighbors cajoled in her living room, her mind began assessing them one by one.

Lisa: Age – about twenty-eight. She was a little on the chunky side, with well-developed breasts, and a very young face. Attractive despite the extra poundage, she was articulate, with a vocabulary to be marveled at. Highly intelligent, and with a clearly enlightened perspective, she sounded like a social worker.

<u>John</u>: Age – thirtyish. Very tall and way too skinny to be good-looking. He likely had acne as a teenager, as his complexion was loaded with deep, reddened pock marks. Also educated, but not as sharply intelligent as his wife, he seemed more the follower type then a leader. He also smoked an awful lot. Even his clothes smelled of tobacco. He owned a somewhat strange sense of humor that easily brought laughter to a room. A nice enough guy, indeed, but not the type one would be instantly drawn to in a crowd. Dierdre wondered how he found someone such as Lisa. They seemed particularly incompatible.

<u>Steve</u>: Black and in his early twenties, if that. If a musician could have a particular look about him, he was a prime specimen. His 1970s afro-style hair was thick and unruly, and his fingers were particularly long and thin. Dierdre considered how skillful these hands might be at playing piano or guitar, or any other instrument for that matter. He thought nothing of lighting up and then passing a joint in her apartment, which made her a bit uncomfortable, but she tried to ignore it. He had a somewhat abstract way of thinking that she found refreshing. Steve was both intriguing and amiable.

<u>Marion</u>: She was about the same age as Dierdre, and was one of the tallest women she had ever seen, topping six feet for sure. She also had large breasts, curly, orangey-red hair and a heavy-boned, athletic build. She was striking, with a super white smile that served as her most attractive and compelling feature. She talked about sex a lot. She seemed proud of what appeared to be an abundance of sexual experience for someone still so young. Surprisingly, Dierdre couldn't help liking her too. Something about Marion was very real and honest. Her enthusiasm and optimism towards life was infectious.

While they were quite a diversified lot, Dierdre's housemates certainly seemed sincere enough in their attempts to make her feel welcome at the brownstone. She liked them and they, in turn, appeared to like her as well. She couldn't recall having enjoyed the company of others in the past as she had enjoyed the company of these relative strangers that first evening at the brownstone. Just two days after escaping the heartbreak of her adolescence, fate had gifted her with potential friends and for that she felt truly blessed. Her life was already changing so quickly, and this time it seemed for the better. It felt good.

Chapter Ten

The week went by quickly. A great deal needed to be done, but Dierdre's energy level was so high that by the time the weekend rolled around she was very satisfied with all she had managed to accomplish.

John was having a pot party on Saturday night, and Dierdre accepted his invitation with great hesitation. She never experimented with drugs and didn't know that she wanted to start now, but how could she not go? She lived there. Assuring herself that she would not actually have to smoke the stuff, she recalled the bragging of her high-school classmates. Who smoked, who snorted, who popped, who shot up. On the heels of the 60s and now in the 70s, drugs were cool and so was anyone who did them. She guessed she just wasn't cool. Saturday night would be her formal introduction to being cool and she prayed she wouldn't make a fool of herself. She prayed something would come up and John would cancel the party. She prayed to come down with a bad case of the flu so she would have an excuse to stay safe and secure in her own place. More than anything, she prayed that the cops wouldn't come and raid the place. Jail was definitely not cool.

At well after 10 p.m., guests began dropping in at the brownstone. Arriving at a party before dark, Dierdre realized, was also not cool.

John didn't bother to greet anyone at the door. Rather, the majority of visitors knew exactly where to go. Dierdre watched from her east window as they arrived, some two-by-two, some alone, and still others in groups of four and five. How did John plan to accommodate all of these people in his small apartment? Over twenty people had entered the brownstone within just the past hour. What would Mr. D. say about all of this? Surely, he would object. If the illegal drugs weren't enough of a reason to be furious, the issues of fire-safety regulations, loud music disturbing the peace, and the neighbors, surely was. Shaking her head in amazement, Dierdre contemplated what the deceased Mrs. D. would think of it all. "Surely, she would be turning in her grave this very moment," she said as her thoughts were disrupted by a sudden, hard-fisted knock on the door.

When she answered, there stood Marion, clad in baggy jeans and an oversized, sleeveless sweatshirt. She held a reefer. "You're missing a terrific party. Come join in girl, John grew the pot himself. Super potent stuff. Must be that special plant food he's been using."

Dierdre was nearly intoxicated by the sickeningly sweet smell that wreaked in the hallway. Beyond Marion's statuesque body, she could see people everywhere. They were sitting on the staircase, leaning on the banisters, and even hanging out the windows. John may have been providing the high, but clearly the accommodations were quite literally "on the house."

Oh, God, let there not be any undercover cops here, she told herself, as the invitees began to infiltrate her spotlessly clean apartment. Two total strangers came in first, followed by Lisa, Steve, then more strangers. Coming and going, back and forth, in and out. The heady stink of pot was everywhere, even in the bathroom.

I hope these people don't have anything contagious, she thought. They say you can get VD from a toilet seat. She wanted them all to leave. She wanted to disinfect the place. She wanted to disappear into the floor and walls of her own apartment. Squeezing through the crowded hallway in an attempt to get outside for some fresh air, nearly everyone she passed offered her a drag on their reefer or fingertip full of snuff. In a courteous fashion, she refused them all with a casual, "thanks, I'm good for now," accompanied by a tight-lipped excuse for a smile.

When she finally approached the front door to the brownstone, she caught a glimpse into the half-open door to Mr. D.'s apartment. How could anyone have the nerve to invade the landlord's suite? Good God, someone was in there. Do something! If Mr. D. returned to the smell of pot in his own home they would all be evicted for sure.

Resolutely, she marched headstrong toward what was still a concealed view of the intruder, white-socked feet stretched casually on the foot rest of Mr. D.'s recliner.

"Excuse me, but can I help you?" she asked, as she grasped and turned the chair to meet with the mystery man face-to-face.

"No thank you dear, I'm doing just fine."

"Mr. D'Angelo!"

There he sat, amidst a huge cloud of weed smoke, happy as a lark, eyes glazed.

"Mr. D. What are you doing?"

"I'm rolling another smoke, dear," he answered quite matter-of-factly. "Come sit here with me and we can share this one." Dierdre reflexively sat at his command.

She must surely be asleep and having a very strange dream. Maybe due to the hot and spicy enchiladas she ate for dinner. She couldn't believe her eyes. The poor, departed Mrs. D. would surely die all over again if she witnessed this.

"Why do you look so shocked, dear?" Dierdre realized that her mouth and eyes were frozen wide open at the sight of him. Mr. D. appeared quite the expert at reefer rolling as he licked the thin, white paper and sealed it methodically with his fingertips.

"I'm sorry," Dierdre apologized. "I guess I'm just not quite used to the city way of life. Do you folks do this often? Don't you worry about what the neighbors will say?"

"Little Dierdre, all of the neighbors are here," Mr. D. slurred. "You are so sweet and unspoiled, Ms. Dierdre. Like a little girl."

"I'm sorry," Dierdre apologized again. Why am I always apologizing? She thought. She sighed and said, "I suppose I am very naïve about many things. I've never really fit in too well."

"Have you ever tried this?" Mr. D. asked as he proceeded to light the just-rolled smoke.

"Well, uh, no."

"Do you want to try it?" he asked. "I can show you how. I'm kind of new at it myself. Only tried it for the first time this past spring when I started renting rooms in the brownstone, but it's not hard. Here." He handed a smoking, flattened object to Dierdre and beckoned her to try it. What the hell, she decided, and took a short drag on her first reefer.

Dierdre and Mr. D. took turns slowly smoking the pot until only the tip remained. She feared she had turned absolutely green from the stuff, but soon found that her head was becoming lighter with each inhalation, and that left her with an oddly pleasant feeling. He coached her along, telling her went to inhale, when to hold her breath, and when to exhale.

Unbelievable. One week after running away from home and she was being coached by a senior citizen on the proper way to smoke weed.

The party continued for hours. The last of the guests headed home well after 3 a.m. Dierdre hadn't mingled much. She rather enjoyed hanging out with Mr. D. and listening to stories about when he was a much younger man. The other tenants must have been amused by Dierdre's choice of a party companion, she thought, but she really didn't care. The hallway and stairwell stank of smoke. Dierdre feared for her apartment. Trudging up the stairs, she felt woozy and her legs were heavy. She was trying desperately not to vomit. All she wanted to do now was to lie across her sofa bed and rest her head on a soft, plush pillow.

When she reached apartment number five, the lingering odors of pot and tobacco greeted her. Oddly, the studio was nearly as clean and organized as she had left it earlier that evening. Nothing appeared to be missing (a roomful of strangers could have cleaned her out of her already minimal personal belongings). Apparently, this was not a pilfering crowd. She supposed the folks in the neighborhood simply enjoyed getting high together. Why did she always have to be so suspicious and untrusting?

Too tired to move, Dierdre forced herself to open the sofa, not bothering to shed her clothing. By the time she stretched out on the bed, her drug-intoxicated mind was spinning with thoughts and ideas. She imagined that Mr. D. was very lonely since the death of his wife of over fifty years. Perhaps he rented these apartments in an attempt to surround himself with fresh and eager minds. Experimenting with pot was, maybe, his attempt at reliving his own youth, rediscovering life, or avoiding growing old. A part of her felt sad for him, while yet another part admired him. Great courage and strength was required to accept being suddenly alone after experiencing a lifetime of loyal companionship with another. He must have loved his wife very much. He had spoken so kindly of her. She was gone now. His children and grandchildren moved to other states, leaving the brownstone and the people in it as his family now.

Dierdre felt comfort and satisfaction in having spent this time with Mr. D. She hoped that of all of his tenants, he liked her the most. In many ways, Dierdre and her landlord were quite alike. They were both in discovery phases of their lives, he for the second time and she for the first. Sometimes, discovery was frightening, but it was also exhilarating and enlightening. Smiling, she turned over in bed and tucked both hands beneath her pillow. Her head was still weightless from the pot, but also lighter was the feeling in her heart as she fell off to sleep. Freedom-week number one was now over and she had done okay, actually, better than okay. She had done splendidly, and she couldn't wait for what tomorrow would bring. One week ago, she was the "bit-part extra" of the Farrell family. On a hot, summer's night at the brownstone, her newfound spirit of adventure earned her a supporting, and perhaps, eventually, starring role in the up-and-coming "Emancipation of Dierdre."

Chapter Eleven

The first summer went well. Dierdre loved her job at the publishing company. She enjoyed dressing up for work each day. Everyone who worked in the city did. Never having been a follower of fashion fads, in time, she soon found herself dressing with the posh of a city girl. She loved the feminine, yet assertive, look of the other women in her office. A few months ago she would have compared them to her sister, all appearance and little brains, but the city girls were different. Most were intelligent, educated, self-determined, and self-assured. Many of them were also alone and struggling to survive, to be independent, to need no one. They lived their lives to satisfy themselves and no one else. City girls had an "anything goes" approach to life. Getting drunk, stoned, or bedded was perfectly acceptable. Yet, it remained just as acceptable to be sober, to stay at home and read a good book on a Saturday night, to choose to spend time with friends, or to choose to be alone.

For the first time in her life, Dierdre felt attractive. Male coworkers and even strangers on the street sometimes turned their heads when she walked by. She was often ill at ease with their hungry stares, but was also flattered.

Dierdre and Marion became inseparable that summer. They shared mutual interests in the arts and literature that afforded them many afternoons and evenings visiting museums, libraries, and the theater. By summer's end, they had become the best of friends. Dierdre made no contact with the Farrells since the day she fled from the family home. They didn't know where she was and probably couldn't have cared. As a result, her paranoia had substantially diminished. The brownstone hosted many a hot, summer night's party and, likewise, neighboring apartment houses did the same. Every day seemed better than the day before.

Days turned into weeks and weeks into months. The fall and winter holidays came and went – – Thanksgiving, Christmas, New Year's. Dierdre's popularity soared during this time, and the party invitations were overflowing. Maybe a little popularity wasn't so bad after all. While she still cherished her privacy and the peaceful, quiet moments that her small studio afforded her, she learned that to have fun sometimes was okay, too.

The winter rapidly became spring and before she knew it, Dierdre was celebrating her first anniversary at the brownstone. She made many friends during her first year away from home and that felt good. She hadn't thought about her family in a very long time. Although she still harbored many childhood fears and insecurities, she had done her best to make conscious efforts to overcome them. The "Emancipation of Dierdre" was now well into its second act, and Dierdre was the star. She felt in control now. She had already been promoted once on the job and a second advancement was shortly forthcoming.

She spent her leisure time either exploring the arts with Marion or quietly exercising her own abilities at creative writing. She also volunteered with the city's Humane Society. How she loved caring for and playing with the shelter animals. So many dogs and cats of all shapes and sizes lived in the sanctuary, all with beautiful souls, and all alone and afraid, much like she would have been for the better part of her life, were it not for her beloved Max. Indeed, she missed him terribly, and would surely never forget him. Yes, her horizons had significantly widened as a result of living in the city. So much was here to see and do, and she was determined to see and do it all.

Relationships with men were still off-limits, though. Young men made passes at her from time to time, but a well-rehearsed and tactful manner of turning down offers for lunch, dinner, and movies enabled her to retain relatively good working relationships with the guys in her office, despite her rejections of them. Although Dierdre was growing prettier with each passing season, even the growing sense of self-confidence that fine clothes and pricey makeup afforded her could not help her to feel comfortable with a man. Too many afternoons alone with Daniel Farrell had seen to that. Every man reminded her of him, in some way. The way they walked, the way they talked, and mostly the way they stared. Every man posed a threat to her self-esteem. Every man ultimately wanted just one thing from her, and she wasn't prepared to deliver.

Conversely, Marion was quite sexually active and far from shy about discussing her many exploits with the opposite sex. Dierdre found her friend's stories quite amusing. Most amazing was Marion's ability to so explicitly describe the details of her sex life. Dierdre had not experienced, nor could conceive of the physical and emotional pleasures that Marion so eloquently described. She tried to imagine the waves of pleasure and ecstasy, but found it impossible. Sex was all about pain and degradation. She never told anyone about her father. Not even Marion. All of her friends believed she was untouched, and Dierdre chose to convince herself of the same.

Despite the great progress she had made in that first year, sometimes she was still so confused. A part of her cursed her naïveté and inexperience, while yet another part found shelter and security in it. The world Dierdre imagined was still so far from that of reality. If only she could find a way to bring the two worlds together. She didn't know how or where to begin.

Chapter Twelve

Marion persuaded Dierdre to enroll in a night course at City College the following fall. She enjoyed being surrounded by a group of people who shared an interest in perhaps her greatest love, writing. The class was composed of thirty students, most of them women. The handfuls of men were ordinary looking. All except for one.

Paul Wellington was different. His tall, hard body was more athletic than intellectual, and his blonde, sun-bleached hair was significantly shorter than was the current trend. He sat quietly in the back of the room, listened intently, but never spoke. Dierdre couldn't help but stare at him during class. He was incredibly handsome and her face reddened on the occasions when his deep, blue eyes caught hers before she could turn her head away.

Other female classmates were apparently attracted to him as well. Many approached him to make idle conversation during the regular ten-minute break in the second hour of the three-hour class. Like a ritual, the professor would call for break at exactly 8 p.m., and everyone would casually leave their seats and shuffle into the hallway for a quick cigarette and conversation. Paul always migrated towards the foot of the large stairwell. Night after night, Dierdre watched as he pulled a Marlboro out of his chest pocket and lit it (always with a match, never a lighter). With arms resting on the banister, he proceeded to smoke with short, quick puffs. Women approached him attempting to make flirtatious gestures or to elicit propositions. Paul smiled graciously during these conversations, but from their fallen faces, not a one of the ladies got lucky.

Every now and again Paul's eyes would meet Dierdre's from across the hall, but neither approached the other. Dierdre felt bewildered, not so much by Paul's failure to flirt with her, but more so by her unusual and unprecedented desire for him to do so. Cute guys at the office were of no interest to her. So what about this man attracted her so? She knew nothing about him except his name (which she determined was as pleasant sounding and appealing as the rest of him). What she did know, however, was that she looked forward to Monday nights at City College more and more, and often took special care to freshen her clothing and make-up before class.

Dierdre did some of her best writing during that semester. The professor found her to be quite talented and often chose her stories to read in front of the class. "Fresh, stylish, and mature" were the words used to describe her work. The acceptance played well with Dierdre. Her compositions meant a great deal to her, for they represented the only way she knew to bring her beloved world of fantasy into the real world of the written word. Story-telling provided the bridge that connected the dreams and the realities of her life.

Paul was always the first to lead the classroom applause after recital of one of Dierdre's tales, at which point he would turn to her and smile. As the semester wore on, Dierdre came to look for his gestures of approval more and more, but after ten weeks, words had still not been exchanged between them. Only brief glances, quick smiles and strange, unexplainable vibrations that could be felt from across the room.

As many times as she thought about it, Dierdre wouldn't dare approach him. What would she say to a relative stranger anyway? What was someone like Paul doing in a class like this? From where had he come? How old was he? What was his occupation? Was he married, engaged, or divorced? Most of all, why did she even care to know?

She wished she knew how to flirt. Marion would certainly have wasted no time in going after a good-looking hunk of a man like Paul

Wellington. But she wasn't Marion. She was Dierdre, naïve with regard to matters of the opposite sex, and petrified at the thought of being touched by a man. Fleeting glances made her nervous enough. She could just imagine her reaction if he actually came over to talk to her.

As the end of the semester neared, she so wished that he would. She sensed a unique sensitivity and vulnerability that went deeper than his strong and athletic physique. She recalled how her initial analysis of the brownstone residents turned out to be incredibly accurate as she came to know them better. She wondered how well she could dissect Paul.

Paul Wellington – In his mid-to-late twenties. Occupation? The short hair and solid body were indicative of someone in the police force, or perhaps the military. He was definitely not the desk-job type. He seemed intense and private, much like herself, and clearly preferred to listen rather than to talk.

She didn't even know him, but yet, she liked him. Yes, she liked Paul Wellington, and despite her fears and inhibitions, she wanted to get to know him better. Only a few sessions remained. In a few more weeks the semester would end and then their paths might never cross again. It was now or never. She wasn't prepared to handle either.

Chapter Thirteen

The last four weeks of the semester were long ones. In addition to daytime office hours and the usual night-class workload, Dierdre spent almost all of her remaining leisure time crafting the short story that was required as her final exam. Her mind was filled with ideas, but she had difficulty deciding on a storyline, and the words didn't seem to flow as smoothly as she would have liked. When the tale was completed, however, she decided that she was relatively happy with the final results. The quality of her work was, indeed, far from best-selling material, but being a novice writer, she chose not to be so hard on herself.

Dierdre arrived at school to turn in her final paper with feelings of anxiety. After this night, she would most likely never see Paul Wellington again, and despite all of the unspoken glances, she remained afraid to utter even the most casual "hello." She was pathetic. She noticed Paul a few yards ahead of her as she walked down the lengthy corridor to room 316. He had a very purposeful walk. His broad shoulders and stiff posture gave him an enviable aura of strength and confidence. She observed his every motion and carefully examined every aspect of his masculine, yet sensual strut.

God, he is gorgeous, she thought, as Paul entered the classroom to stand in line behind two other students.

Dierdre entered in line behind him, being particularly careful not to stand too close or to brush up against him. Embarrassed by her attraction to him, she hoped it wasn't obvious.

The five-minute wait in line seemed like forever. Others were chatting back and forth, but Dierdre and Paul remained silent. Standing close, and with his back turned away from her, he was even taller than he appeared from a distance. She couldn't quite identify the cologne or aftershave he was wearing, but she knew that it wasn't a typical one. The men at work drowned themselves in a variety of obviously commercial fragrances, but not Paul. His aroma was fresh, clean, and subtle, just like everything else about him.

When Paul's turn came to deliver his paper, the conversation with the professor was cordial and brief. With a "thank you" and a handshake he turned to leave. He didn't even look at her. Trying desperately to conceal the disappointment that crept onto every inch of her face, Dierdre forced a smile for the professor. He praised her previous work and expressed his expectations regarding what he believed to be "a very promising literary future if she just stuck with it." Somewhere in-between his self-praise for the discovery of her rare talent and his well-wishes for continued achievement and success, Dierdre caught a glimpse of the papers neatly stacked on the table's edge. *The Sea of Dreams, by Paul Wellington,* sat atop a pile. Only half listening to the continued ramblings of the professor, Dierdre couldn't help wondering about the theme behind Paul's story. Then reality sunk in. She gazed towards the doorway. Paul was gone. It was too late now to say "hello," to find out where he came from, how old he was, if he was married. She had blown it. The only man who had ever made her head turn (and for reasons that she still couldn't comprehend) had walked out the door and out of her life. A sick feeling knotted her stomach as she bid farewell to the professor and turned to leave. As she approached the doorway she could still smell Paul's light, yet lingering manly fragrance. She would never forget the earthy smell of him, the scent of this man who was apparently destined to remain a stranger. She wished she could turn back the clock. She wished to be more like Marion. Mostly, she wished she didn't wish that she always wished to be someone else.

At times like this, Dierdre realized she still had such a long way to go to free her body and soul from the torments of the past. She feared the task was an impossible one, a task that was and would remain beyond the realm of her ability to accomplish. As she frantically searched the college hallways for perhaps one last glimpse of him, she finally forced herself to accept that Paul was nowhere to be found. In frustration, Dierdre walked slowly through the dark, half-empty parking lot to the car Mr. D. so kindly lent her on school nights. While rummaging through her purse in a desperate effort to find her keys, a sudden tap on the shoulder nearly startled her out of her boots.

"Looking for these?" a soft, deep voice asked from out of the dark.

She turned quickly, shaken by the surprise. There, in the flesh, dangling the car keys before her very eyes, stood who Dierdre would, henceforth, deem her "perfect stranger." Paul.

Chapter Fourteen

"You left them on one of the desktops while we were waiting in class," he said. "Don't suppose you would get too far without them." His still outstretched hand beckoned her to take the keys.

Dierdre blushed, and her mouth was frozen half-open. Her feet stayed stuck to the pavement.

"Well, since you aren't in any hurry to get home, what do you say we have a drink?" Paul asked, smiling as his blue eyes pierced right through her.

Realizing that she probably look like a fool, Dierdre tried to speak but no words came. She tried to move but felt paralyzed from head to toe. Paul reached for her right hand and carefully placed the keychain in her open palm. "Maybe another time then," he said, as he turned to leave.

"Oh, no, tonight is fine!" Dierdre blurted.

A few seconds after the words were spoken she recognized the voice as her own. Oddly, she hadn't even felt her lips move, but knew that she had managed to turn them into a smile as Paul made an about-face towards the car. Grinning back, he was obviously pleased by her decision.

They took Paul's car, a metallic blue '67 Mustang convertible, to a small café in the center of town. Dierdre fidgeted in her seat during the drive, and her palms were sweaty. She was nervous about being alone in the car with him. After all, she really knew nothing about this man. Paul played the stereo softly as they drove through the brightly lit, though cold, city with the top down. The heater was on high and the cold, crisp, evening air blew through their hair. On the second week in December, the Village shops will gaily decorated for the holidays. Christmas lights, angels, wreaths, and anxious shoppers were everywhere. The beauty of the season made for casual and pleasant conversation during what could have been an otherwise uncomfortable ride.

The café was dimly lit and with a rather quaint, European décor. The menu included everything from wine and cheese to quiche, Italian cheesecake, and international coffees. A live, folk guitarist played soft, romantic tunes in the distance that gave further charm to this warm and cozy restaurant. Paul ordered a scrumptious dinner for two including hot antipasto, fettuccine alfredo, and a not-too-dry chardonnay. Dessert consisted of strawberries and cream and cappuccino, all of which was topped off by a soothing, full-bodied, blackberry brandy. The food and drink alone were enough to make the evening special, but the intriguing company was the cherry on the cake. Paul's invitation for a brief, after-class drink ultimately became a glorious night on the town that went well beyond any of Dierdre's expectations. They talked the night away. Paul was, perhaps, among the most interesting people Dierdre had ever met. He was in his mid-twenties and was working as a Merchant Marine.

Bingo, I was right, he doesn't have an office job, Dierdre thought, once again extremely proud of her analytic abilities.

His stories of other peoples and cultures were fascinating. In just four years, he traveled more than half-way around the world and to some of the most exotic places imaginable (the Mediterranean, the Middle East, and even South Africa). Dierdre also discovered that he had studied Marine Biology, which came in handy in his current occupation. She was also fascinated by the sea-research studies in which he was currently involved, most recently, investigation into the mating rituals of giant sea turtles. Indeed, his high-spirited adventures included everything from overseas trade escapades to whale-saving demonstrations. Paul spoke affectionately about the character and strength of the ocean and all of the glorious creatures that dwelled within its depths (the stingrays, sharks, dolphins, and more). He spoke of the oneness with nature that he experienced as a mariner and the spiritual freedom that was unique to his way of life. He also spoke about his love of writing and playing the guitar. One day, he would use words and music to tell the world all that he could about his greatest love, the sea.

Although Paul Wellington had already had enough experiences to last one-hundred lifetimes, and Dierdre felt unsophisticated and raw in comparison, all she wanted was to hear more about his life and his exploits. Likewise, though, Paul wanted to hear about her life too. He coaxed her to talk about herself, but with limited success. Their hours of conversation remained light-hearted in nature, concentrating largely on their mutual love of story-telling, in all its forms.

It was 2 a.m. when Paul drove back to the college. They were both tired from the food, wine and talk, but it was a good tired. They entered the now-empty parking lot at well after 3 a.m. Dierdre suddenly realized that she had never stayed out alone this late before and thoughts of worry and concern on the part of Mr. D. and her friends crossed her mind. She imagined them thinking that she was in an auto accident, or worse, that she was mugged or kidnapped. She felt guilty about her insensitivity and selfishness. She should have called someone from the café, but was just too engrossed in Paul and hadn't even thought about it when it counted. How would she explain this to them? She pondered the question as the Mustang pulled up alongside Mr. D.'s rusty, old Rambler.

"Can I see you again?" he asked, staring at the steering wheel as he spoke.

"Sure. Why not?"

"Great. Then I'll call you, "he said, smiling at her in a way that suddenly made her uneasy. "I'll call you if you give me your number." He looked at her, waiting for some response.

Turning to an empty page in one of his notebooks and pulling a pen from his shirt pocket, he handed her both, as Dierdre's body turned numb again. What was wrong with her? She was just fine in the restaurant and when the car was moving, but a fear swiftly crept up inside her. That same feeling of panic that being alone in the house with her father always gave her. Would she never be free of him?

With another urging from Paul, Dierdre nervously scribbled her phone number on the open page. She was shaking so much that she could barely write and hoped that her handwriting would be legible. Scrutinizing what she had written, with a smile, Paul closed the notebook and tucked it carefully under the driver's seat.

"If you want, I'll start your car and we can sit here for a while until it warms up a bit?" he asked.

Sit here while it warms up. Was this the moment of truth? All evening long he was careful not to touch her, careful not to be too assertive. Now what? What if he wanted to kiss her?

She was afraid to even think about it, all the while knowing that she would probably make a fool of herself since she didn't know how to kiss even if she wanted to. She decided at that very moment that she didn't want to.

Paul let himself out and quickly stepped to the passenger side to open the door for her. Embarrassed by her inexperience in moments such as this, Dierdre uttered something about "having a wonderful time" as she grasped her car keys from out of her purse.

"Let me," he said, as he took the keys from her hand, unlocked the driver's side door of the Rambler and opened it.

Dierdre sat in the car with the door still open, placed the key in the ignition and turned it. Paul wiped the light frost from the windshield with his bare hands. He closed the door for her and beckoned her to open the window with a light tap on the mirror. As the window slid half-way down, he playfully kissed and pressed his still wet fingertips to her nose, then waved her on. Shivering in the cold, his arms folded tightly against his chest, he watched as she drove slowly around the parking lot dividers and out the main gate.

Dierdre shook all the way home. Was her trembling caused by her emotional state or by the fact that she had forgotten, in her tenseness, to turn on the car heater? She still knew so little about Paul. As open as he was about his profession and his love of writing and music, she sensed that something deeper lay beyond the surface of this man. Something he purposely chose not to speak of.

Real typical, Dierdre scolded. You go out with a guy once, your first date ever no less, and already the guy has some deep, dark secret. Like maybe he's a criminal, or maybe he has two wives and eight kids out there somewhere. When are you going to get real, Dierdre? Maybe he's just a really nice guy. Maybe he likes you. Maybe all men don't keep score cards of sexual encounters and brag to their friends about their conquests. Maybe you're just being paranoid again, as usual.

As she pulled up to the brownstone, the house was dark and still. She made every attempt to enter as quietly as possible so as not to wake any of the tenants. She wasn't in the mood to explain where she was until 3 a.m. on a weeknight.

"3 a.m. on a weeknight! Oh, God. I have to get up for work in less than four hours!" she moaned, as she acknowledged her return to the real world.

She rolled into bed and couldn't keep her mind off Paul. She hoped she didn't blow it with the aloofness of her farewell. She hoped he wasn't an escaped felon. She hoped he really meant it when he said he would call her, and soon. Mostly, she hoped that if and when he did call, she would have the courage to see him again. With mixed feelings of fear, confusion, and light-hearted delight, she fell off to sleep with the smell of wine, fettuccine, and Paul Wellington oozing from every fiber of her being.

Chapter Fifteen

P aul didn't call until three weeks after New Year's. Believing that she had totally screwed up their first date, Dierdre was surprised to hear from him, but she had thought of Paul often during the holidays. Many an evening she found herself wishing he would call and found herself jumping whenever the phone rang in hopeful anticipation. By the time the New Year had passed, she had, for all intents and purposes, given up on the idea of ever seeing him again, so she had difficulty disguising her elation when the call finally came. Ah, the sound of Paul's voice! After several hours of conversation with which they caught up on things since their last date, Paul finally asked if he could see her again. Without hesitation she said, "Yes!"

For the next two months they spent a great deal of time together. As each day passed, Dierdre became more comfortable in his company, but on the few occasions when Paul attempted to hold her hand or to put his arm around her shoulder, she couldn't help but squirm. Confused, but sensitive to her apparent anxiety, Paul made a conscious effort to keep things on a platonic level. This was hard for both of them, though, particularly since an undeniable physical attraction clearly existed between them. Save for an occasional reflexive touch on the hand or knee, he was careful not to invade her physical space.

Although Paul was hard-pressed to understand why Dierdre seemed so uncomfortable when he touched her, he wasn't confident enough in the solidarity of their newfound friendship to push the issue. Leaving well enough alone for now, he determined, was his best course of action. She seemed naïve in many ways. Yet, there were times when she seemed to possess a certain philosophic wisdom well beyond her years. So filled with contradictions was this girl that despite his previous experience with women, Paul was puzzled. Although her body remained unquestionably cold to his touch, he believed that Dierdre's heart was warm for him. Her teetering between child-like innocence and grown-up strength and maturity lent a certain unpredictability to her actions and reactions. Paul was never exactly sure what to expect from her. He was scheduled for ship duty on the first of April and would be out to sea for the next four months. All he could do was hope that Dierdre would still be there when he returned.

To the contrary, Dierdre found Paul to be quite predictable. He walked and talked in a manner that expressed confidence. He loved to talk, joke, and tell stories. He enjoyed his life so, and Dierdre wished that she could learn to love hers as much as he seemed to love his. Her heart hurt at frustrating him. She often wondered why he continued to hang around at all. He was a man who could have any woman of his choosing. In fact, she couldn't understand how some woman, somewhere, hadn't managed to sink her claws hard and deep into such a great guy. Many women had surely tried.

Ship duty for many months per year would put a lot of time and distance between a couple, and after less than two months of his company, Dierdre knew that she would miss him terribly when he set sail in the spring. Would he still be interested in her when he returned? Could she find the courage to allow herself to be touched by him in a way that goes beyond friendship? He was so patient and understanding now. Would he be so when he returned? If he returned? She considered that he might just be a real ladies man. Perhaps she was just one of one-hundred women that he had wined and dined. Maybe he was a sailor with a girl in every port. So what if she wouldn't let him touch her. Plenty of other women would sleep with him in a minute. Perhaps he genuinely just deemed her a friend with common interests. She refused to admit that she wanted him, that she enjoyed the touch of his hand, and the look of longing and desire in his eyes that inherently brought back memories of a day in time she so desperately wanted to forget. Damn Dan Farrell! And damn her mother and her sister! She cursed them all because each in their own way had maimed her ability to give of herself to others. A lonely young woman needing desperately to love and be loved, she prayed for help. But most of all, she prayed for hope.

Chapter Sixteen

In the last few weeks before his departure, Dierdre and Paul had become inseparable. The brownstone tenants couldn't have been happier for Dierdre. Surely, they had never seen her as carefree and blissful about life as she was since she met Paul. Mr. D. called him "a nice young fellow," and Marion deemed him an "absolute hunk." John and Lisa reminisced with Dierdre about the wonder of their dating years, and Steve whistled silly love songs in her ear every chance he got. Sometimes, the sweet, almost sickening smiles of these charming people embarrassed her, but the sincerity of their delight in this new relationship overwhelmed her with a unique sense of joy and love that she had never before experienced. For the first time in her life, Dierdre belonged to a family of beautiful and thoughtful people. So what if they smoked weed and did cocaine on occasion. So what if they each had flaws and eccentricities. Most people did, and Dierdre was no exception. The important thing was that they truly cared about her, and found unselfish pleasure in her newfound sense of self-esteem and self-confidence. Paul was good for Dierdre and everyone knew it. He made her feel attractive and desirable. By respecting her need for physical space between them, he also made her feel safe.

Dierdre had grown so much in the past two years and she was a better person for every experience. She loved her home, job, friends, and new way of life. The butterflies in her stomach and warmth in her heart were new feelings that made her feel good all over. Paul made her feel good all over, great all over, happy all over. She wanted him. There was no denying it. And she believed that he wanted her too. Was this what it felt like to fall in love? If so, it was magnificent!

All of the signs were there including a face that absolutely glowed. She tried to convince herself that Paul was a mere infatuation, and that she became overwhelmed with emotion for him because he treated her better than she thought any man could, because he told her she was pretty. She felt safer believing that her feelings for him weren't real but, rather, just imagined. Yet, every morning when she awoke her first thoughts were of Paul, the same warm thoughts that carried her off to sleep and filled her dreams each night.

How could this be happening to her? How could she let herself fall for a man who she knew had to leave her? She still had so much to learn about Paul. In many ways, he was still quite the stranger. A few months was hardly enough time to become familiar with even the little things about him, such as if he took cream and sugar in his coffee, the title of his favorite book, the music he liked to listen to or play along with on his guitar. She knew little of his past, his family, or his friends. Surely such a young and vital man must have friends in many places. What about his family? As curious as Dierdre was about Paul's somewhat mysterious life, she didn't dare ask him about his past for fear that she might prompt him to inquire about hers. She would do anything to avoid bringing back to life the years of rejection and the ultimate disgrace that she had so desperately thrown out the window and stuffed down the sewer with her blood-stained panties. And what deep, dark secrets might Paul have? Everyone had secrets and likely he had them too. Was he as curious about her past as she was about his, but also being careful not to unlock the pain and heartache of a time long gone in his own life? Dierdre couldn't imagine what it could be, but she sensed that Paul was hiding something. As kind and attentive as he had been in her presence, she could swear that his mind, and perhaps a piece of his heart, was someplace else. Somewhere that, despite his fondness for her, she simply could not go.

In what felt like merely a single day, Dierdre had met, befriended, and possibly grown to love this "perfect stranger." On the first of April she found herself waving good-bye to him from the pier. As he waved back, she prayed that this was only a temporary farewell, one that promised his return and answers to the numerous questions that filled her mind about him. She tried to have faith and was determined to be ready. She had four months to get her act together. If she hadn't lost him already, she was prepared to take whatever steps necessary to ensure his future return. She surely wouldn't let him forget her and promised to write every day. He promised to do the same, as well as to bring home a boatload of assorted souvenirs from every European and African port.

With a lump in her throat, Dierdre waived until the ship was nearly out of sight. She had so much to do and no time was soon enough to begin. Determined and purposeful, she made a quick about-face off the pier and rapidly made her way to the Rambler. She missed Paul already, and couldn't wait to get back to the comfort of her beloved new family and friends.

Chapter Seventeen

The springtime bloomed beautifully that year. Dierdre couldn't help feeling the joy of the season, the pleasure that in a few short weeks previous to natures reawakening, Paul had taught her to appreciate in a way that she had never done before. Although he was half a world away, she didn't feel alone. Letters from Paul came regularly, adding to her sense of confidence in his feelings for her. An abundance of gifts were sent from every port of call. Jewelry, books, and articles of clothing were among them, but what she treasured most were his letters. Paul had such a vivid way of describing things. So eloquent were his words that miles between them seemed to disappear between the lines of his dramatic and colorful verses. Through his poetry and verse, she could actually taste the salt air over the Atlantic, feel the warmth of a sunset in Greece, and take pleasure in the smiles of the children from Spain. She could share all of Paul's experiences in her own heart, and that made the bond between them seem even stronger.

As the weeks progressed, Dierdre began to feel more relaxed about Paul and the security of their feelings. Determined to make some radical changes before his return, she began with a visit to the best beauty salon in town for a blonde highlighting of her naturally, honey-colored hair and a soft body wave, both of which brought out a sensuality and sophistication in her youthful face that she never knew existed. Oddly, the subtle changes made her look more like her sister, Daryia, than she ever dreamed possible. She wasn't sure if that was good or bad, but the abundance of compliments she received was music to her ears. She hoped Paul would also approve. She would have dyed her hair purple if she thought it would make him happy.

The change in her hair was only the beginning of her transformation. Dierdre began jogging daily in order to get her already slim figure firmer and shapelier for the summer months. It was torture at first. Running half-way up the street left her dry-mouthed and breathless. She persevered, however, and soon was running nearly five miles per day. Admittedly, becoming so concerned with her physical appearance was strange. For perhaps the first time, Dierdre understood and empathized with her sister's obsession to always look fabulous, and how important a woman's appearance could be to her own self-esteem. Although she hoped she would never be as shallow as Daryia, she liked her new look and the attention she received as a result. She wasn't going to beat herself up about it.

In addition to the physical changes, Dierdre continued her intellectual pursuits. Paul encouraged her to take another course in creative poetry that truly suited her current, dreamy and philosophic state of mind. Upon Paul's insistence, Dierdre copied him on every piece of work she completed, all of which he gave rave reviews. With each word of encouragement from him, her abilities flourished. Dierdre wasn't sure if she was truly talented, or if falling in love was the key to the growing sensitivity in her writing. She only knew that her style suddenly shifted from the hard-lined cynicism of the past to a warmer, more idealistic tone. This was a change that Dierdre decided she could easily get used to.

As if all of this transformation wasn't enough, Dierdre realized that she also had to come to grips with her own sexuality, or the lack thereof, and face her fears. What had become of her family? She imagined that Daryia would have snagged some unsuspecting son of a doctor, lawyer, or wealthy businessman by now. If so, she likely had the wedding of the century, at everyone else's expense, of course, but surely she must have made a beautiful bride. She pictured her sister in a long, white dress of pearls and lace, with a train that went on forever. She imagined her laughing and smiling for photographers and then wondered how anyone could possibly survive being married to Daryia for any length of time.

Face it, she thought, the guy would have to be a saint to last even a week.

Were her parents still together? They had so little in common and clearly whatever relationship they had seemed horribly strained when last she saw them. God only knew what became of Daniel Farrell. Was he still teaching, or had his drinking made that totally impossible now? His alcoholism surely robbed him of his physical as well as mental health, and he proceeded to take the entire family down along with him. And what of her mother?

Suddenly, Dierdre recalled the pain that burdened her heart, mind and body. She remembered the high-school graduation to which no one came, the forgotten birthdays, and the despair of losing her loyal and beloved dog, who she laid to rest unaided. Mostly, she recollected the pain of that Saturday morning in June. She could still see the bruises on her arms and face, still feel the pain of the ultimate violation that fate had forced upon her. She couldn't handle it then. She was too young and too afraid, and so she ran away rather than face up to it. She fled to a place where, by the grace of God, no one could find her.

Caring and respectful friends offered her a sense of personal worth that her family couldn't manage to encourage in themselves, much less anyone else. Yet, the past had indeed followed her. She couldn't erase it. She couldn't pretend that the earliest years of her life and the incestuous assault never happened. She considered a support group, and even a psychotherapist, but determined that exposing the deep, dark secrets of her past to total strangers wouldn't change anything. She was so confused. Although Paul never pressured her into intimacy, his frustration was often apparent. Dierdre couldn't let him go on believing something was wrong with him, and that she didn't want him, when her body surely ached for his touch. She cringed at the hurt and uncomprehending look on Paul's face whenever he attempted to kiss her with an open mouth and she abruptly turned her face. His deep sighs and pursed lips expressed sadness and disappointment, more so for his inability to melt the coldness of her body than for the unsatisfied throbbing of his own. She hated when she rejected him for he was, without question, the best thing that had ever happened to her.

Dierdre tried to imagine what it would be like to make love to him. Could he evoke in her the waves of pleasure and ecstasy that Marion so vividly described? Oh, would that her spirit could be as liberated as that of her best friend. After many weeks of soul-searching and concerted prayer, Dierdre realized that the only way to lay the pain and heartache of the past to rest was by facing it head on. If she searched deeply enough, she could find the courage that was necessary to truly set her free.

Chapter Eighteen

The air was unusually humid on the last Sunday in June as Dierdre headed out for her early morning run. Typically, she jogged for two miles in the park, then traveled another mile or so along the boulevard to the deli where she bought the morning paper on her way back to the brownstone. The sun on her face warmed her all over.

Paul would be home before she knew it and she couldn't wait to see him. She missed him so much. Practically flying up the stairs, Dierdre was back in her apartment before 7 a.m. She tossed the newspaper onto the kitchen counter, brewed her morning coffee, and then hopped into the shower. She looked forward to putting her feet up and relaxing as she read the Sunday paper each week.

The coffee smelled strong, but she liked it that way. Dierdre reached for her cup with one hand and the daily with the other, and leaned back against the large, floor pillows that faced the east window. There wasn't much good news. Stocks were down and the cost of living was up. The unemployment rate had risen and so did the number of people living in poverty. Drug use was also on the rise. No big surprise there.

She continued to lazily scan the pages for articles of interest. Quite by chance, she came upon the obituary section that she determined was particularly lengthy in this edition. Out of curiosity, she began to read them.

Thelma Waters – Eighty years young, from cancer. Leaves behind her loving husband, Richard, and two sons, Mark and Dennis. Reposing at Bartlett's Funeral Home.

Michael Domingo – Suddenly, at the age of seventeen. Leaves behind his parents and six brothers and sisters. A funeral mass will be held followed by interment at Holy Sepulcher Cemetery on Tuesday.

Sandra Bergman – Beloved mother of Mary, Stephen, Louis, Alexander, and Ethan. Beloved wife of the late Jaime. Holocaust survivor whose life knew both the joys of love and the horrors of hate. Rest in peace. You will be missed. From your friends at the 3rd Avenue Synagogue.

They went on and on. Death had no prejudice. It visited the young and the old, the rich and the poor. To the infirmed, it was likely a blessing, but to the young and healthy, who met with untimely death by a mere stroke of fate, surely it was horrific. What about the lives of these souls and spirits who were no longer here on earth? Likely, they all had family and friends who loved them. She thought that, if nothing else, our very existence was validated by the love of others. In the big picture, loving and being loved was all that really mattered.

With that thought in mind, she turned the page and suddenly her heart felt as though it would fall from her chest.

Daniel Farrell – Loving husband of Louise. Beloved father of Daryia and Dierdre. Professor of sociology for twenty-five years and member of the Lion's and Rotary Clubs. Reposing at Mallory Funeral Home. Interment at 10 a.m. on Monday at Jefferson Memorial Cemetery.

Was she dreaming? Could it be true? Was her father really deceased? She reread the piece as if scanning it a second time would somehow change something. She was shocked and yet not at all surprised. He had been killing himself with alcohol for years. The obit made no reference to the cause of death, but Dierdre couldn't help wondering. She felt cold and her stomach went queasy. Her father was dead. She had wished it on him so often since the attack, but the knowledge that he was really gone gave her no satisfaction whatsoever now. Had the years truly softened the pain of his assault after all? Her feelings of despair were unexpected, and she couldn't help feeling sadness at his passing. Suddenly, he didn't seem like a monster, but only a sick and lonely man who, for some reason, had given up on his own life. She wanted so much to understand what could have brought him to such an abysmal place. She wanted to say that he deserved to die, that the Grim Reaper should have called for him years before, but she couldn't. All she could feel now was sorrow, and giving into the feeling, she cried.

After a few moments, she looked at the obit again, and noticed that she was named in it. Odd, she thought, that the family would acknowledge her in any way. She considered they did so for appearance's sake. She simply didn't know. What she did know, however, was that she couldn't hide forever. The time had come to face the past and all of the pain that went along with it. She had nothing left to fear. Indeed, she had an entirely new life now. Her father was gone and couldn't hurt her anymore. No one could. What she needed now was to know the truth. To know how her father had died, why she had been so physically and emotionally abused as a child, and why her family found it so hard to love her.

Without further reflection, she rose and took haste to the bathroom to brush her hair. She studied her image in the mirror and saw a completely different woman from the one who looked back at her two years ago in a dark and lonely hotel room. This person was a smarter, stronger, and more hopeful woman. Yes, she was better and happier than she ever thought she could be, because she loved a man who believed in her. More importantly, she finally believed in herself. No one could take that from her.

Chapter Nineteen

With a thousand thoughts running through her mind, Dierdre pulled a navy pantsuit and a pair of black pumps from the closet. She dressed quickly, and with her jacket still draped over her arm, ran downstairs to Mr. D.'s and asked to borrow the car. As always, he obliged.

Driving to the suburbs would take nearly two hours. The Rambler didn't have air conditioning, and within minutes of getting in the car, she was dripping with sweat. Dierdre wasn't sure if her heavy perspiration was from the heat or her nerves, but she felt some relief when she got to cruising to 55 to 60 mph with the windows down.

The traffic was light. She had left the brownstone quite early and people who enjoyed sleeping late on Sundays were likely still in bed, save for the early church goers. As she drove down the freeway towards a place that she used to call home, her heart was racing. She must be crazy to be returning to the emotional turmoil of her childhood. Yet, she knew that she had to conquer the demons of her past before she would be free to unearth the blessings of the future.

She reached the funeral parlor just after noon. Dierdre didn't recognize any of the cars in the parking lot. Odd that she would assume she might after having been gone for so long. She parked in the most distant section from the entrance to the building, which hadn't changed a bit. In fact, most of the town hadn't transformed much at all. Did her old house also look the same? For a brief moment, she contemplated riding past it to check it out. No. Being in the old neighborhood brought back a lot of memories, though, and she tried to picture the rest of it in her mind. The school yards were only a mile away, and the mall three or four miles farther up the road. A stationary on the corner of Bertram and Cedar faced the McDonald's across the street from the Chevy dealership. If she strained she could see the storefront of the grocery where she used to work. It was still open for business. Dierdre wished she had fonder memories of this town. Unfortunately, she had spent most of her time here wishing only that she could leave for what she hoped would be a better place.

As she observed the funeral director raising the American flag, Dierdre's thoughts turned to her beloved dog, Max. He was such a treasure. She wished that she could put some flowers on his grave and hoped it had remained undisturbed since she laid him to rest. She recalled how much she enjoyed having a pet, and hoped someday she could have another. Max was her best friend for the longest time and she found comfort in knowing that she would love and remember him always.

Dierdre glanced at her watch. Almost 1 p.m., and the parking lot was still relatively empty. Perhaps the viewing didn't begin until the evening hours. With great hesitation, she tentatively entered the funeral parlor. A tall, light-haired gentleman in a dark suit met her at the building entrance. "Good afternoon, ma'am," he said. "You must be here for the Farrell viewing. It's the only one we have today."

Dierdre nodded." Yes," she said. "He's my father." So strange to say those words.

In a gentle voice the director said, "Visiting hours don't actually begin until 2 p.m., but your father is ready and you are welcome to go inside now if you would like." With a sympathetic smile he escorted her down a long hallway to the viewing room and then excused himself.

Dierdre stood frozen at the entrance. Was she really here? Alone again with her father? She was always so afraid of being alone with him. The soft glow of amber-colored lighting reminded her of the hotel in which she had sought refuge two years ago. While it should have been comforting, it wasn't. Dierdre swallowed hard, trying desperately to muster up the courage to step inside. A headache teased at her temples and a sick feeling grew in her stomach. With a deep breath and her eyes half closed, she forced her feet to move. By gradually placing one foot in front of the other, she managed to take five or six steps. Finally, she passed the partition that separated her from what remained of the man that was her father.

Ever-so-slowly, she moved closer to the bronze-colored, metal casket until she found the courage to open her eyes fully and gaze upon him. Her heart sank. He looked significantly older than a man in his mid-forties. The lines on his face were like battle scars that even the mortician's make-up couldn't hide, and his hair, which was only slightly gray when she last saw him, was now totally white. His lips seem to bear a permanent frown, despite apparent efforts to curl them upwards, and his folded hands appeared stiff and wrinkled.

Making the sign of the cross, she knelt before him. With tears in her eyes, she recited the Lord's Prayer softly under her breath. She wanted more than anything to hate him right now and to believe that his soul was burning in Hell for what he had done to her, but all she could feel was pity. Perhaps God was testing her ability to feel compassion for this man who assaulted her in a drunken rage and stripped her of her innocence. Had God forsaken them both on that horrible day in June? She didn't know. All she knew was that it was time for forgiveness and with absolution would come the healing that she so desperately needed. Dierdre prayed a Hail Mary and an Act of Contrition over him and arose.

"Rest in peace, Daddy," she said, wishing that in some way he could hear her. "For whatever it's worth, I will try to forgive you."

Slowly, she lifted her head and turned to leave. With eyes still wet with tears, she came upon her mother.

Chapter Twenty

Mother and daughter looked upon each other in silence for several minutes. Although Dierdre's appearance had changed quite dramatically since they had last seen each other, there was no change in Louise Farrell. Dressed in black from head to toe, she was still strikingly attractive. Slim and well-coiffed, she remained vibrant and youthful-looking. They stared at one another, looking deeply into each other's eyes, each holding their breath, waiting for the other to break the ice and speak the first word.

"Hello, Mom," Dierdre whispered.

"Hello, Dierdre," her mother sighed.

As Louise glanced over her daughter's shoulder to catch a first view of her husband's lifeless body, her body tensed.

"It's been a long time, Mom. What happened?" Dierdre asked, all the while not certain that she wanted to know. "How did he die?"

"He killed himself," Louise declared, almost matter-of-factly, but looking away from her daughter's intense gaze as she spoke.

"What! How? Why?" Dierdre's heart beat heavily in her chest.

"Why does anyone take their own life?" Her mother responded. "He drank himself into a coma and died. It wasn't the first time he tried it, you know. He's been wanting to kill himself for years. It was only a matter time before he would succeed. He didn't want to live. He was a very unhappy man."

Dierdre turned to face the coffin and look once again upon her father's corpse. She had always believed that alcohol would be the death of him. Turning back towards her mother, she asked, "Do you know why I left so suddenly, Mom? Do you know what happened to me?"

"Yes, I know," her mother answered.

Her response was so muddled that Dierdre wasn't certain she heard her correctly, but her jaw dropped just the same. "I don't understand," she said. "You knew that he…"

"Yes, I knew," her mother repeated. "I knew for a long time. You see, he had done the same to me."

Dierdre swallowed hard. "You mean Daddy…?" Desperate for an explanation for so many of the events that led to this moment in time, Dierdre begged, "Please, Mom, explain all of this to me. I know that we didn't get along very well, but I need to know the truth. Why was Daddy so sad? Why were we all so unhappy? Why was there so much hurt? And why do you all hate me so much?"

In what was an oddly maternal gesture, Louise Farrell took hold of her daughter's hand and led her to a small sofa towards the back of the visiting room. During her childhood, her mother's touch was reserved for hitting her when she was ill-behaved, and so the comfort she felt from it was strange and unexpected. Dierdre looked over her shoulder at the casket once more, and breathed a sigh of relief at putting some distance between them and her father's body. Moments before her mother's appearance, Dierdre was intent on searching for a way to forgive the man for his sins against her. Now she wasn't so sure that she wanted to.

As they sat down beside one another, Louise held her daughter's hand tightly in hers. "I suppose it's time that you know the truth. The truth about all of us."

Dierdre's eyes were now wide. Was she going to regret what she was about to hear? She listened intently as her mother took her back to another place and time.

Louise Farrell was an only, late-in-life child of Doris and Edgar Cunningham. The owners of multiple high-end rental properties in the northeast, they were swimming in money. This affluence afforded them great power and influence in their community, and it was well within their means to give their daughter the best of everything. Louise lived a charmed life and wanted for nothing.

Her parents were overprotective, though, and as a result Louise was rather inexperienced about life when she began her freshman year at a private East Coast university in 1952. The 50s were an exciting time, however, and she looked forward to the freedom that living away from home would afford. She was determined to enjoy as many new experiences as she could. She became one of the most popular girls on campus with great ease. Young gentlemen often showered her with attention. Never at a loss for a date on a Friday or Saturday night, she quickly learned the value of charm and how to use it to her advantage.

Daniel Farrell was in his senior year. He was especially tall and not bad looking for the intellectual, non-athletic type. Being from a lower-middle class Midwestern family, he was socially out of his element in this environment, and wouldn't have been there at all if not for an academic scholarship. Introspective and a loner, he was far from popular.

Louise and Daniel met when he was assigned as her sociology tutor. He, like all the other young preppies, became quickly enamored with her pretty face and warm smile. Louise made it abundantly clear early on, however, that the relationship would never go beyond that of friendship. A relatively poor boy from Iowa simply wasn't her type, and never would be.

By the second semester, Louise became deeply infatuated with the captain of the lacrosse team. Well-muscled and broad-shouldered, Christopher Fields was gorgeous personified, and she spent every waking hour thinking about him. Louise was thrilled when he eventually asked her out. Daniel shared a dorm quad with Chris and didn't like him at all. Also a senior, Chris was cocky and self-absorbed, and had a reputation for being quite the ladies' man. Daniel worried a great deal about Louise, and didn't like the fact that she was dating Chris. He knew that in the end her heart would be broken, although he couldn't say or do anything to stop her. Louise had a mind of her own, she was crazy about Chris, and that was that. Daniel decided, however, that he would keep an eye on her just the same.

The months passed and the spring of 1953 was forthcoming. Louise and Chris were inseparable the entire semester and, on numerous occasions, had declared their love for one another. She lost her virginity on Valentine's Day. Chris was the man she felt destined to marry, and she was happy to have discovered her womanhood with him. She was failing most of her classes, but didn't care. She and Chris were in love, and nothing else mattered. She couldn't wait to bring Chris home to meet her parents, and to announce him as her fiancé. Louise hoped he would present her with an engagement ring before his graduation day so that their intentions could be made official. She anxiously anticipated showing off both the man and the diamond to all of her friends back home. She was the luckiest woman in the world.

Her period was due on or about the first of May, but two weeks went by and it didn't come. Louise convinced herself that she was late because of the stress of final exams, but as each day passed she became more concerned. She and Chris had relations often and rarely used protection. He would just tell her not to worry, and so she believed him. She would believe anything he told her. She had mixed feelings about possibly being with child. Pregnancy and childbirth scared her, but thoughts of a life growing inside of her conceived from their love made her feel warm and cozy. What was she worried about? Chris loved her. He would surely be happy about the baby. The pregnancy wouldn't change their plans. They would be engaged before his graduation and married before she would begin to show.

Louise couldn't have been more wrong. Her pregnancy confirmed, she informed Chris of the pending, blessed event on the day before commencement. He never showed up. Instead, he disappeared like a phantom and she never saw him again.

Louise didn't know what to do. She was afraid to tell her parents. They would be so angry with her. They believed she was still a virgin and women just didn't openly admit to having premarital sex in the 50s. Abortion, illegal at the time, and not to mention unsafe, was out of the question. Besides that, despite his abandonment, she still loved Chris.

She still wanted the baby that was growing inside of her, a child that she believed was conceived out of love.

In great despair, she confided in her friend, Daniel. His heart ached at her pain. Wanting more than anything to help her, he offered to marry her. He suggested they elope. No one would ever have to know that she was pregnant before marriage or that the child was not his. He promised that he would love and care for them both, forever. He hoped that in time, Louise would learn to love him as well. Louise believed that she had no other options. After all, her reputation was at stake. She had no romantic feelings for Daniel, and doubted she ever would or could, but he was a kind and decent man. Ultimately, she agreed to marry him with great trepidation and a heavy heart.

The Cunninghams were not at all pleased with their daughter's choice of a husband. They saw Dan Farrell as a common, country boy whose background and upbringing were far removed from theirs, but the deed was done, and all they could do was accept it. Daniel got a job teaching high-school social studies and his salary was barely enough to support a wife, not to mention a baby. As a result, upon the announcement of Louise's pregnancy, the Cunninghams gave them the money they had put in trust for their daughter's college education to help them buy their first home. The marriage was never consummated. Louise made perfectly clear that she and Daniel would never have a real marriage. She didn't love him in that way, and while she appreciated his willingness to help her, all that really mattered to her was the child she was carrying.

Daryia was born on Valentine's Day, 1954. Louise thought it ironic that her first child was born on the anniversary of the day she lost her innocence to Chris Fields. She saw so much of him in the baby's hypnotic, green eyes. Despite everything, she never stopped loving him. She wished so much that Chris was her husband, and that together they could raise this beautiful little girl. Daniel, on the other hand, saw only Louise in the face of this baby. He fell in love with her from the moment he saw her, and wished that she was his. He also wished that Louise would allow him to love her in a way that a man should love a woman, but she would never let him touch her.

For the next several years, life revolved around Daryia and she quickly became quite spoiled. Louise lived for the child, and her parents followed suit, providing her with all of the extras that Daniel's teaching salary could never afford them. Just as her mother before her, Daryia didn't want for anything. Daniel and Louise were successful at hiding the truth about Daryia from the family and everyone believed that Daniel was her natural father. No one ever knew of their marriage of necessity, or of Christopher Fields. Yet, Daniel yearned for a real marriage. He desired a woman who loved him, and would make love to him. He wanted so much for Louise to be a real wife, but she would have nothing of it. And so Daniel Farrell began to find solace in a bottle. His alcoholism progressed slowly, but steadily. The days, weeks, and years of rejection and despair ultimately became too much for him to bear, and as time passed, he began to lose himself in liquor. He didn't seem to care, and neither did anyone else.

Dierdre listened intently as her mother spoke of the past. She finally understood why her sister was so adored by their mother. Daryia was conceived by the only man her mother had ever really loved. She owned the same deep, green eyes of the one who stole their mother's heart, and ultimately broke it.

"But what about me, Mom? What about me?

By the time Daryia was a toddler, Daniel was already drinking excessively. Louise was well aware of the problem, but as long as the bills were paid and she had Daryia to love, nothing else mattered. She and Daniel became more estranged with each passing day. With each of her husband's attempts at intimacy, she pushed him further away.

Louise was still only in her early twenties. She could attract a man like a bee to honey, and she knew it. In short order, she began having extra-marital affairs. She made no attempt at hiding her exploits from Daniel. Just because she refused to be intimate with him, didn't mean she was about to become a nun. Louise felt that her affairs were justified. She never promised to love Daniel, or to be a wife to him in the true sense of the word. She made it abundantly clear that so long as Daniel was discreet, he too was free to seek the company of others. She believed they were both too young to simply wither up and die. If he wanted to kill himself with booze, that was fine with her. Louise wasn't about to let life pass her by because of a few wedding vows that, although she had spoken, she never really meant.

Louise arrived home at 2 a.m. on a hot, August night after an evening out with friends. Daniel had fallen asleep on the living room couch. An empty bottle of vodka lay beside him. Louise looked at him with disgust as she proceeded to her private bedroom to undress. As she slowly peeled off her clothing, she was grateful for having left Daryia with her grandparents for the evening. Daniel wasn't responsible enough to care for the baby when he was drinking, and he was doing that more and more. With a sigh, she closed the door and fell into bed. She was half asleep when she heard him enter the room. She usually locked the door, but had forgotten that evening in her haste.

"Daniel, get out," she moaned, annoyed at his disturbing her sleep. He said nothing.

"Didn't you hear me?" She asked. "I said, get out! Get…"

He was on top of her repeating over and over again, "I love you. I love you. Love you."

She tried to fight him off, but couldn't. Within minutes he had violated her, and then, just as quickly, was gone from the room. Nine months later, Dierdre was born. Louise remembered wanting to kill him. She recalled how much he disgusted her and how the drinking had turned him into such a monster, someone she didn't know.

"I hated him so for touching me," she said. I hated him for impregnating me, and that's why I hated you. That's why I cursed you from the moment you were conceived and began growing in my belly. If it weren't for your sister, I surely would have killed myself."

Dierdre was speechless. So many things were becoming clearer now, but she was uncertain that she wanted to hear anymore. Her mother openly declared hatred for her, and it hurt to hear her admit it.

"My father was a horrible man!" Dierdre exclaimed as she peered towards the coffin.

"No," her mother answered. "He wasn't a horrible man. He was a man who helped me when I had no one else. A man who kept my secret for a lifetime, and took it with him to his grave," she said as her eyes also shifted towards the casket. "He was a lonely man. All he ever wanted was to be loved, but I was incapable of loving him back. I wasn't a wife to him. I wasn't even a good friend to him. So he drank to mask the pain, and I let him do it. I took no responsibility for him, just as I took no responsibility for you. Your father was a very desperate man. I knew what he was doing to you back then. I knew, and didn't do anything about it because I didn't care enough about either of you. After he violated me I never slept another night without locking the bedroom door. He would wander through the house at night trying to get in, but couldn't. That's when he started lingering behind your door. When he started watching and walking in on you. A good mother would have stopped him. A good mother would have told you to lock your door and wouldn't have left you alone with him so often. I protected your sister, but I didn't protect you. I did have guilt about it, you know. I was relieved when you left two years ago. I only wished you had managed to leave before he violated you too. It was an awful thing to have happened. Take pity on your father. He wasn't a bad person. He was just a very sick and lonely man, and he did love you very much. He never wanted to hurt you. He just wanted someone to love. He died because he couldn't forgive himself for what he had done to you."

Dierdre's mind was racing with so many thoughts that her head began to pound. "Do you hate me now, Mom?"

"No, Dierdre. I don't hate you. I'm your mother, but I don't really even know you."

"No, you don't," Dierdre said, with tears spilling down her cheeks. "And I'm not at all the same person that I was two years ago. Not at all the same."

"Are you happy?"

"Yes, I am."

"That's good. You deserve to be happy. Your father would have wanted that."

Dierdre's mother looked at her watch. Almost 2 p.m. The guests would be arriving soon. "I'm glad you came, Dierdre. I didn't know where you were, but was hoping that you might, per chance, see the obituary and come when you saw your name in it."

So her mother placed the obit in the paper. She wanted her to come. She wanted to confess the truth after a lifetime of lies.

"Will you be all right, Mom?"

"No." Her mother cried, throwing her face into her hands.

They walked one last time towards the casket and together gazed upon Daniel. "I hope you can forgive me." Dierdre placed her arm around her mother's quivering shoulder in an effort to comfort her. The welcome display of kindness brought a tear to her mother's eye.

Dierdre didn't know how to respond. She wanted to offer forgiveness to both of her parents. She believed that doing so would make her a better person, and bring healing to her own broken spirit, but surely that was easier said than done.

Chapter Twenty-One

With a heavy heart, Dierdre bid farewell to her mother. Voice shaking, and unable to look her directly in the eye, she promised to stay in touch. Similarly hesitant, her mother agreed to do the same. With a final nod, Dierdre took her leave, marching rapidly from the visiting room and into the parking lot.

She sat in the Rambler for quite some time. She didn't really know for how long, only that it seemed like forever before she put the key in the ignition and turned on the engine. With both hands firmly holding onto the steering wheel, she gazed out the window into the street. What now?

She drove around the block two or three times before she realized she had been traveling in circles. A few minutes later, she found herself at the dock. She parked the car, and walked to the edge of the pier. The waters were turbulent. The fast-moving, rolling whitecaps so reflected her own feelings of apprehension and confusion, and the ominous clouds overhead served only to darken her mood further. Her stomach was queasy and she wanted to vomit. The visitation, and seeing her mother for the first time in years, left her uneasy and confused. Her heart raced. Her head hurt. And most of all, her soul was in a quandary. She couldn't change the past. Like it or not, it was an integral part of her. Of the person she had become. There was no denying that. Yet, she didn't want the pain of the past to eat up her present and future. Could she let go of the hurt? The fear? The shame?

As the skies opened up and the thunder rolled, a hard and steady rain suddenly crashed down upon her. Quickly, she raced back to the Rambler in an effort to find shelter from the storm. Soaking wet and shivering, she jumped into the driver's seat, threw her head in her hands and wept inconsolably. She cried out for her friends. For Paul. The only people who truly made her feel safe and loved. She knew that she needed to return to her new way of life as quickly as possible. If letting go of this pain was at all possible, the remedy was not in looking back, but in discovering what lay ahead.

Dierdre clinched her jaw and gritted her teeth. She quickly started the car, and pulling away from the pier, as if by magic, the storm suddenly ended as quickly as it began. With the sun peeking through the now dispersing clouds, and more determined than ever, she headed home.

Chapter Twenty-Two

It was 4 a.m. on the second Saturday in July when Dierdre was abruptly awakened by the repeated rings of the telephone. She picked up the receiver to a familiar, light-hearted voice asking, "What are you doing for breakfast?"

The immediate recognition of his tone startled her to consciousness. "Breakfast? Paul, is that you? Where are you?"

"On top of the world, Sugar," he teased.

"Really Paul, where are you?" She couldn't hide the anxiousness in her voice. Paul wasn't due back for nearly two more weeks and Dierdre couldn't imagine from where in the world he could be calling.

"What's the matter, aren't you hungry?" He continued to tease her, laughing under his breath.

"Paul, I swear if you don't get serious and tell me where you are I will absolutely scream."

"Okay, I'm at the pier. One of our stops was canceled at the last minute so they sailed us on home."

Her heart was pounding so hard that she could barely breathe. Paul was home. She couldn't believe it. He hadn't deserted her after all. He promised he would return and made good on his word.

"So what do you say to breakfast with a ship-worn, sweaty, and starving seaman?"

"Oh, yes! Don't you budge. Stay right where you are. I'll be there before you can say scrambled eggs. Will meet you on the east side of the pier. Oh, God, Paul, you're home. I can't believe you're home."

"Well, hurry up and get over here, woman! I have a surprise for you that will knock your socks off."

"A surprise? What surprise?"

His being home two weeks early was enough of a surprise. Dierdre couldn't possibly imagine what could bring her more delight then just seeing and being with him again.

"You'll see," he said laughing. "You'll see," he repeated, and the receiver went suddenly dead.

Dierdre never moved so fast. Within minutes she had showered, washed her hair, dressed, and put on a quick face. As she prepared to rush out of the house, she realized that she needed to borrow the car from Mr. D. It wasn't yet 5 o'clock in the morning, but there was no time to waste. Paul was home. He was waiting for her with a big surprise. She could barely stand it.

Frantically, she ran into the hallway and pounded on Marion's door. Still half-asleep, Marion answered in a half-growl, agreeing to apologize to Mr. D. for Dierdre's taking the car without asking in advance. She waved and said "Go for it!"

Dierdre sped to the pier in record-breaking time. As she entered the main gate, her heart was beating so fast that she feared she would hyperventilate. Over and over again she told herself to maintain some sense of self control. She couldn't appear too desperate and enthused about seeing Paul again. She didn't want to scare him away. She turned into the east side of the pier and within seconds caught a glimpse of his long, muscled, jeans-clad body in the distance. She wasn't dreaming. Paul was really home. He was home and waiting for her on the pier.

Upon sight of the Rambler, Paul waved frantically with both hands high over his head. Having parked as close to the dock as possible, Dierdre ran up the pier to meet him halfway. The briny saltwater filled the air, and the warm summer breeze kissed the exposed skin on her arms, legs and face. It seemed that the distance between them would never be breached, but soon they stood motionless, and only inches apart.

With a huge smile, Paul stretched his arms out to her. "How about a hug for travel-worn sailor, Sugar?"

Their embrace was long and warm, and the kiss that followed expressed a great deal more than friendship. Dierdre hoped that Paul felt as good at this moment as she did. The loving smile on his face was proof that he did.

"So where is my surprise?" Dierdre asked in an attempt to ease the slight embarrassment she felt as a result of her own physical responsiveness. "You don't think I drove all the way over here at this ungodly hour just to watch the sunrise do you? Where is it?"

She began peeking in his shirt and pants pockets in a teasing fashion, unaware that she was arousing him further. He kissed her again, this time softly on the cheeks and hair. His strong hands gently cupped her face. The sun was beginning to rise rather suddenly now, and as the skies grew brighter, his senses became increasingly more awakened to the essence of her. Dierdre's hair had grown well past her shoulders since he had seen her last. Soft and inviting, he impulsively twirled it between his fingers and leaned over to breathe in her scent. She returned his display of affection with a child-like smile.

Pulling away from her ever-so-slowly, Paul took both of Dierdre's hands in his and squeezed them firmly.

"You're full of surprises, Sugar. And so beautiful. I'm not so sure now that my surprise can top yours," he said, as his blue eyes scanned her lean and fit figure.

"Does this mean that you're not going to knock my socks off?" She joked, innocently unaware of the unseemly connotation of her words.

Paul broke out into a hearty laugh. "Sugar, I would be happy to knock your socks off anytime. You just say the word."

He was still laughing as Dierdre's face turned a bright red upon realizing what she had said. "Oh, I didn't mean it like that!" she said. "You knew what I meant."

Dierdre was so embarrassed that she suddenly wished she could become invisible. And yet, before she knew it, she was laughing too, so hard that it gave her the hiccups, which served only to prolong their shared merriment. By the time they finally composed themselves, they had been on the pier for nearly an hour and the sun was full up.

"It's good to be home," Paul said as he put his arm around Dierdre's shoulder and led them off the pier.

"It's good to have you home," she replied.

For the first time, Dierdre realized that to Paul part of being home meant being with her. Suddenly, the word "home" was beginning to take on even greater meaning. For now, "home" was more than just the brownstone and the people in it. Now, being "home" meant being with Paul, someone with whom she felt safe and secure, loved and desired, and where, most of all, she could feel free enough to laugh at the humor in herself.

Chapter Twenty-Three

They drove to the nearest diner for breakfast and spent over two hours sharing enough food and coffee to feed an army. They had so much to talk about. By 9 a.m. they had eaten and talked so much that their jaws were tired. The day was shaping up beautifully. The sun was never so bright, and despite the 85° temperature, the dryness in the air made the heat comfortable. A splendid day to spend outside, Paul insisted they do just that.

He paid for the meal and led them back to the Rambler. "Are you ready for your surprise?"

"I've been ready since early this morning," Dierdre answered, tapping his chest. "This had better be good, sailor, or I'll send you back out to sea."

"Oh, it's good all right." He grinned.

"Well, what is it?"

"Can't tell."

"What! Why not?"

"Got to show you."

"Why?"

"Because it doesn't fit in my shirt pocket, that's why. Boy, you tell a girl you brought home a surprise and all of a sudden she gets so demanding."

"Okay, fine then, don't tell me. I don't care anyway. I'm not a material person."

"You mean you really don't want to know?"

"No, I don't care. I really don't care."

Paul smiled and said, "Okay, okay. I'm being a real pest, huh?"

"You could say that," she answered, refusing to look at him.

"I'm really sorry, but I'm telling you the truth. I have to take you to see it. Can you be patient just a little longer?" He took her hand and leaned over to kiss her softly on the brow.

Turning toward him with a smile she said, "Okay, sailor, my day is yours. But where are we going, Paul? Where are you taking us now?"

"To Heaven, Angel. Heaven on earth."

The ride out east was a true pleasure on such a picture-perfect day. The sun was shining brightly, and the cloudless sky was a vibrant, cyan blue. The sound of birds chirping and singing their sweet summer songs filled the air. They headed for the tranquility of the seashore, which was miles away from the hustle and bustle of the city. Paul and Dierdre sang aloud to the songs on the radio and talked and laughed during the commercials. Within just a few hours since their reunion, they felt as though they hadn't been separated at all. As if Paul had never left. As if they had always been as close as they felt at this very moment.

Despite the distance, the drive seemed to go quickly, and within what felt like merely minutes, Paul parked at the most beautiful marina Dierdre had ever seen. The sails on the boats were a rainbow of colors, and happy, smiling people seem to dance with joy as they leapt on and off the various crafts.

"Oh, Paul, look at it. It's fabulous!"

Smiling, Paul led her onto the boardwalk for a closer look. The air smelled sweet and clean, and the sun beat warmly on their shoulders as they walked from one end of the dock to the other, enjoying the peaceful, yet playful atmosphere that surrounded them. Paul enthusiastically explained the mechanics of the sailboats, motorboats, and various other sea vehicles as they walked. So knowledgeable was he, in fact, that Dierdre didn't imagine there was anything he didn't know about sailing, fishing, or the sea. As they continued to walk and talk, Paul stopped at what Dierdre believed to be the most beautiful sailboat she had ever seen. Carefully, he took her hand, leading her onto the pearl-white craft.

"Paul, we shouldn't be doing this. The owners would have a fit if they caught us on their boat," she said, pulling away from him.

"It's okay, he said. "I know the owner. Besides, this is a great chance to show you how it all works."

With some hesitation, Dierdre looked around and then followed him onto the craft. Paul gave her a tour of the boat as he explained every last thing about it from how and why it stayed afloat to the workings of the sails. His eyes flew wide open with excitement as he described practically every nut and bolt that held the vessel together. He knew it so well, he could have built it with his own two hands. Dierdre couldn't help admiring the unrelenting enthusiasm with which he instructed her. And when he brought her to the stern, her face suddenly glowed with astonishment at the letters painted so colorfully there. Slowly and under her breath her lips spelled out the words, "Dierdre's Folly." With her mouth wide open, she turned to him.

"Paul, did you buy this boat? Is it yours?"

Unexpectedly, he turned toward her and answered, "No, Sugar, it's yours. Surprise!"

"Mine? But I don't know how to sail."

"I promise you that by summer's end you'll be the finest sailor, man or woman, in the port. Do you love it?" He asked with arms outstretched and blue eyes gazing up to the heavens.

"Oh, Paul, it's incredible. It's. It's…"

"Want to take her out?" He winked at her, laughing at her sudden inability to speak.

She nodded. "What do I do?"

Well, the first thing you do, Captain, is to put on your sailing cap. Can't leave the dock without it. It's just not proper." He pulled a pure white cap monogrammed "Captain Dee" from under one of the seats.

"I'm the Captain?"

"That's right, Sugar, and that makes me your first mate," he answered with a voice filled with pride. "Ready whenever you are."

She smiled. "Well, okay, but you do promise not to let me sink us, right?"

"Fear not, I haven't sunk a ship yet, Captain," he said, placing his mate's cap onto his short-cropped hair.

Step-by-step, Paul instructed her in every aspect of operating the craft, beginning with pulling out of the dock space, out the inlet, and into the bay.

As they proceeded to open waters Dierdre asked, "When do we put up the sails?"

"Soon. When we catch a good wind and some open waters ahead."

About fifteen minutes later he shouted, "It's time!"

"Time? Time for what?"

"Time to raise the sails, Sugar."

She followed his instructions religiously, wanting to impress him with her quick learning ability and newly discovered sense of coordination. He smiled at her continuously. As they drifted into deeper waters, the pink and blue sails caught a warm and steady breeze that seemed to carry them off into another time and place. Feeling a sense of peace in every fiber of her being, Dierdre lay on the deck with her eyes closed, and her face turned towards the welcoming rays of the sun. As the sails rustled in the wind, perhaps for the first time, she felt part of a bigger and better world. Paul had promised her the most wonderful day of her life, and he delivered. As he came to lay beside her, he rested his travel-weary head on her shoulder.

In a soft voice he asked, "Are you happy?"

"Oh, yes!"

Almost breathless, she realized that Paul had given her something that she had never dreamed possible. He had given her a glimpse of Heaven. And it was beautiful.

Chapter Twenty-Four

They returned to the dock well after sunset. Dierdre hadn't recalled ever feeling so good. As she and Paul locked up the boat for the night, she whispered, "This day has been fabulous, just wonderful! I wish it could last forever. I wish we never had to go back to the real world."

"The night is young. We don't have to go home yet," Paul said in a calming tone that seemed to whistle in the wind." Come on, let's have some dinner. There's a really great place not far from here."

Glimpsing back frequently at the beautiful craft that bore her name, Dierdre stepped to the car with Paul. Arms around each other's waists, they fit so comfortably together, as if made for each other. Paul was so physically strong and solid, and yet his soul was soft and eager to please. The mere nearness of him made her feel things that she never felt before, indescribable sensations that made her tingle all over, made her heart pound with excitement all evening long, and made her desire him in a way that she had never dreamed possible.

Their time in the restaurant was brief, and the dinner conversation limited. After all, what was left to be said when they had come so close to seeing Heaven? Paul's house was located just outside the city limits, and they arrived there well after midnight. Dierdre had only been to his place on a few occasions, and for fleeting moments at best, but she remembered the very lived-in and relaxed decorum. A friend who was housesitting during Paul's tour of duty did a fine job keeping the place in good order, and even washed and waxed his precious Mustang, which reflected the moonglow so beautifully as it sat parked in the narrow, gravel driveway.

"Daddy's home," Paul said, as he gently brushed his hand over the hood. "You'll come in for a while?"

"Well," I do have to work tomorrow," Dierdre said, biting the corner of her lip.

"Call in sick," he told her. "Please."

With a light touch of his hand, she followed him inside as if in a trance, as if the word "please" was a magic word, like "abracadabra," and the stroke of his fingers like the tap of the magician's wand. Part of her was fearful and yet another part wanting. A measure of her desired to turn around and go home, while yet another piece prayed he would ask her to stay the night. Paul gently led her to the sofa, told her to make herself comfortable, and made a quick about-face to retrieve his rather heavy and cumbersome baggage. For nearly thirty minutes she watched as he quietly unloaded piles of dirty laundry, magazines, and other items onto the living room floor. Occasionally, he looked up at her, briefly smiled, and then returned to his mundane chore. She sat on the floor beside him and whispered, "Are you going to do this all night?"

Paul turned to face her and asked, "Did you want to help?"

She shook her head. The silky, now blonde tresses that caressed her shoulders moved in sync.

"Are you bored? Do you want to go home?"

Again, she shook her head from side to side. "You want to stay?" He asked in a tranquil voice, now staring deeply into her eyes, searching.

"Yes. No. I don't know." Her eyes began to tear.

"I would never hurt you. You have to know that."

Dierdre nodded.

"Then why are you so afraid of me?"

He was holding her now, moving his hand softly over her neck and shoulders in a massaging fashion that sent shivers throughout her entire body. She could feel herself trembling. Whether the tremors were out of fear or desire, she didn't know. She tried to remember everything Marion had told her.

"You have to let him know you want him," she would say. "You have to make him believe that you want him as much as he wants you."

"I'm not afraid of you," she answered. "It's me."

"What about you?"

"I don't know how to please you, Paul. I want to, but I really don't know how." She turned away from him so that he wouldn't see her cry.

"And just what do you think you have to do to please me?" he asked.

Dierdre's voice quivered. "Oh, Paul, I was so afraid that you wouldn't come back. I missed you so much. And you've been so good to me. You've given me so much and I've offered you so little in return. I wouldn't blame you if you left and never saw me again."

"I can give you a lot more if would let me, Sugar." He spoke kindly as he held her closer. "If you weren't so afraid of me."

"I'm not afraid of you."

"Then what is it? Please, tell me. Tell me so we can work through it." He held her tighter. "Dee, I want to be with you more than anything, I really do. It's all I dreamt about while I was away. But it's okay if you don't want to. If you're not ready. It's okay." He paused, then added tenderly, "I know you've never done it before."

Dierdre looked at him sharply and in a sudden gush of emotion broke out into such violent sobs that she couldn't stop shaking.

"I'm sorry. Oh, Honey, I'm sorry," he repeated over and over again as he rocked her gently back and forth. "Please don't cry. Listen, we won't talk about it anymore, okay? Whatever it is that's upsetting you about this can wait. It can wait until you're ready to tell me about it. Let's just leave it alone for now."

Despite the great comfort she felt in his strong arms, Dierdre couldn't comprehend how she could possibly tell Paul about her troubled past. Indeed, she had every intention of "just leaving it alone for now."

Chapter Twenty-Five

They spent the remainder of the evening holding one another until eventually they fell off to sleep on the living-room floor. They awoke the following morning to a heavy rain beating against the roof and windows. Realizing that she had cried herself to sleep the night before, Dierdre's initial impulse was to apologize for her child-like behavior. As if he could read her mind, however, Paul simply shook his tousled head, kissed her gently on the cheek, and said, "It's okay, forget it."

God, he's terrific! Dierdre thought, as he continued to hold and kiss her in a loving, unthreatening fashion.

Too exhausted to think about work, Dierdre called in sick, having absolutely no reservations about doing so. A second call to the brownstone followed. Mr. D., answered with his usual morning pleasantries. Relieved that she was safe and in the caring arms of the man she loved, he assured her that he was not in immediate need of the Rambler. As she hung up, embarrassment filled her. What must Mr. D. think might have happened the previous night? Turning back to Paul, she was even more self-conscious about what didn't happen. He must have thought her such a tease. One minute she was making a pass at him and the next she was crying her eyes out. Marion would have been so disappointed in her for failing to seize the moment to discover the still unexplored pleasures Paul had so desperately wanted to awaken in her.

Watching him as he lay with eyes closed beside her on the floor, she wished it were yesterday. That she had the chance to recreate the scene and handle it differently. Paul thought she was untouched. In many ways, she wanted to believe that she still was.

They fully awakened at around 5 p.m. The forceful rain had calmed to a light drizzle, but the sky remained relatively dark and gloomy.

"What time is it?" Dierdre asked, with eyes still closed as Paul leaned over to kiss her.

"They don't measure time in Heaven, Sugar."

"Is that where we are?"

"No, but that's where we can go if you'll let me take you there?" he whispered in her ear and then kissed her gently on the lips.

She could feel the excitement building in him, but was more aware of the eagerness building in herself. His touch felt good. Her body responded to his gentle caress so naturally that it surprised her. Paul's hands moved over her. She stiffened at his initial touch, then gradually melted in the pleasures he led her to experience. Although somewhat tentatively, Dierdre allowed him to undress her. Within minutes, Paul's clothing lay on the floor beside hers. The feeling of flesh upon flesh caused them both to tremble.

"We won't do anything you don't want to do, okay?" He leaned down to kiss her, his hands gently moving down the length of her bare body. Dierdre nodded as her breasts and stomach tingled from the touch of him. As he caressed her further, his warm, wet lips now following an erotic path that his hands had discovered just moments before, Dierdre struggled with her memories of fear and violation. Her body suddenly tightened in response to the recollection of that Saturday afternoon in June. Paul eased up. She caught her breath. If she said "no", he would stop. She felt certain that he wouldn't force himself upon her if she were truly unwilling. She knew that he would never hurt her.

"Are you okay? Do you want to stop?" he asked her, his touch softening but still providing incredible stimulation.

She shook her head, continuing to tremble from the mere nearness of him.

Daniel Farrell, be damned! Her mind cried out as she struggled to push the past aside and return to the present.

She adored Paul. She loved him and had denied him long enough. More importantly, however, she had deprived herself long enough. Today, she was in the arms of a man who loved and desired her, a man who touched her in a way that she had never been touched before. She wanted more. She wanted to be free to experience the Heaven that Paul promised her.

As their passion continued to accelerate with each touch, each kiss, Dierdre soon became lost in the sensuality of the moment. Without warning, and as if by magic, their minds, bodies, and souls became one in the intensity of the waves of pleasure that flowed between them. The swells seemed never-ending, cresting, over and over again, until they were both breathless and exhausted.

"Are you okay, Sugar? Do you know what just happened to you?" he whispered.

Smiling with both satisfaction and relief, she was now tired and limp in his strong arms. "I just saw Heaven?"

"You are Heaven, Sugar."

As Dierdre lay peacefully in his arms, she felt secure in the realization that her days as a "bit-part extra" were finally over. Safe in knowing that on this dark and rainy night in July, a bright and shining star was born from out of a once dark and lifeless sky. She was finally free of the past. It was beautiful!

Chapter Twenty-Six

T heir relationship changed dramatically after that rainy Monday in July. Trying desperately to free herself from the torments of the past, Dierdre believed, perhaps for the first time, that life really could change. She came to realize that physical intimacy had not transformed her. Rather, she experienced an emotional reawakening that resulted from her choosing to forgive the sins of long ago so that she could open her heart to love in the present and future. It felt good to be appreciated, and to be desired with warmth and passion, rather than with cruelty and lust. More importantly, loving in return also felt good. To be secure enough in her own feelings of self-respect to give of herself, body and soul. To belong to someone else and still be her own woman, to give without selling herself out, without losing the sense of identity that took over twenty years to discover.

The remainder of that summer proved to be a continuous affirmation of the lessons that the love and understanding of Paul Wellington had taught her. With each passing day, Dierdre gained courage and strength of character. Everything about her seemed to blossom with newfound life, vibrancy, and joy.

While her attitude had markedly matured during this period, Dierdre also discovered the child in herself. The little girl who somehow missed out on the many pleasures of being young. And as if to put the final seal on a most unfortunate past, Dierdre eventually found the courage to tell Paul the truth about her family and the tragic fate that had befallen them all.

"So now you know everything there is to know about me," Dierdre sighed with relief at the thought that she had no more deep, dark secrets to hold inside of her. As difficult as it was, it felt good to finally tell someone. She was surprised that she could now divulge the story without crying. Indeed, she wasn't at all the same frightened teenager that had been violated so brutally years before. She was a stronger person now than she ever thought she could be, and Paul was the better part of the reason why. Still, she couldn't help but wonder if knowing all of this would change the way he felt about her.

"Are you ashamed of me, Paul?"

He stared into space with tears welling up in his eyes. "Ashamed of you? How could I be ashamed of you? Sugar, you didn't do anything wrong. You were just a kid. An innocent. You didn't deserve any of it. No child does."

He reached out his arms and pulled her close. Melting into his strong, hard chest, Dierdre welcomed his embrace. As she nestled her head beneath his chin and held his hands tightly, she groaned, knowing full well that the sorrows of the past could never be erased just because she had finally found the courage to speak of them. Still, at that moment, all that mattered was the kindness and reassurance of this wonderful man who always knew how to comfort her when she needed it most.

As the weeks of summer flew by, Paul and Dierdre enjoyed many a warm, sun-kissed day entertaining themselves on the Folly. Dierdre became quite proficient at sailing. After all, she had the best instructor, and Paul glowed as she easily displayed the strength, timing, and coordination of an experienced boater. Indeed, Dierdre reveled in this special time together. But more so, she was relieved to have bared her soul about the past, to share the feelings of hurt, disgrace, and rejection that had troubled her for so long. Paul's compassion and support helped her to tear down the walls that she had so steadfastly built around herself. The fortress that had protected her from any further violation and abuse of body, mind, and heart had finally disintegrated. She felt liberated.

As the Labor Day weekend approached, Paul and Dierdre sailed off into the final days of summer with the cool, crisp smell of autumn already filling the air.

"This has been the best summer of my life," she said, as she cuddled close to him. "Will it always be like this?"

"Always, Sugar," he answered, gently brushing the soft, bronzed skin of her exposed shoulders with his caressing fingertips.

"When will you have to leave again, Paul?"

"Not for a while yet. Let's not think about it just yet, okay?"

"Can we take the boat out again next weekend?" she asked. "That is, if it's not too cold."

"Yeah, sure."

Dierdre sensed a frustration and distraction in the somber tone of his voice. "Paul, what is it? What's the matter? You've been acting really weird all day."

"I just have a lot on my mind, that's all," he said.

Dierdre held him closer. "I know that I talk a lot, but contrary to public opinion, I can be a really good listener, too," she said, bringing an almost instantaneous smile to his otherwise pinched and troubled face.

"Would you be very upset if we didn't take the boat out next weekend?" Paul asked tentatively. "There's someplace I'd like to take you. Someone I want you to meet."

"Where? Who?"

"You'll see," he answered, as he played at readjusting the sails to hide his nervousness. Dierdre smiled, eyes flashing. "Another surprise?"

"Sort of?

"A big one?"

"Yeah."

"But you're not going to tell me, right?"

"Right," he confirmed. "What do you say we head for home, Captain?"

"Sure thing, Mate."

As Paul directed the Folly back towards the harbor, Dierdre watched him intensely. Something wasn't right. He was hiding something from her, something that clearly disturbed him. She tried to imagine what it might be. God, please don't let him be married with a wife and a bunch of kids somewhere. Thoughts raced continuously through her mind. Please don't let him be a fugitive from justice, or worse, dying of cancer or anything horrible like that.

She stared at him, evaluating every movement of his muscular body, every expression on his strained face. Observing him gave her no answers, only further questions, doubts and confusion about this man she loved so desperately, and couldn't bear to lose under any circumstances.

Despite her anxious curiosity, Dierdre knew not to press him, or to force explanations that Paul was neither ready nor willing to give. He loved her. She felt secure in that much. With acceptance of his love also came a responsibility to reciprocate the trust and understanding that Paul had so willingly offered to her. Time would bring the answers she sought. Perhaps as soon as next weekend. With that realization, Dierdre on the one hand, wished for the coming week to pass quickly, while on the other, prayed that a miracle would stop time altogether. She feared the revelations that were to come, and could only hope that she had the courage to accept them, whatever they might be.

Chapter Twenty-Seven

The following Sunday was cold and damp, and felt more like October than the first weekend after Labor Day. Throughout the week, Dierdre made whimsical attempts at discovering where Paul was planning to take her. Her frustration increased in the reaffirmation of his uncanny ability to keep her in suspense whenever he so chose. He could be such a mystery at times, a mystery that was often more of a fear to her than a challenge. How could she feel so safe and yet so insecure about him at the same time? She struggled to convince herself that everything would be okay. Paul probably had another very wonderful surprise planned for her, something even bigger and better than his gift to her of the Folly. He couldn't be married with a bunch of kids, or a convicted felon, or dying of some rare and incurable disease. God would simply not punish either of them in such a way that any of those things could be true. She had come too far to be brought back down for even thinking such terrible thoughts.

As Dierdre watched the shiny, blue Mustang pull up to the brownstone that Sunday morning, the blood rushed through her veins. The heavy pounding of her heart continued to beat louder and harder. She analyzed the very uncharacteristic, weary and troubled look on Paul's face as he approached the front door. This sadness that seemed to have fallen upon him very suddenly during the past few weeks worried her. His expression spoke of pain, and it stood between him and all others, including her. She knew that she had to be receptive. She had to force herself to understand regardless of what this day would reveal about him. Empathy and compassion were, after all, what love was all about.

God, please don't let me fail him now, she prayed, as she turned from the window to answer his quiet knock on the studio door.

Greeting him with an overanxious hug and a kiss on his stiffened cheek, Dierdre pressed her body tightly against his, refusing to let go, demanding to hold him this closely forever. Paul's arms never felt so good around her, and perhaps his own sense of need at that moment triggered him to return her fervent embrace with one of his own. When they finally released each other, they did so in silence. Mechanically, Dierdre grabbed her coat with one hand and Paul's waist with the other. She closed the door behind them without looking back.

They drove for the first half-hour in relative quiet. Still unaware as to their ultimate destination, Dierdre bit her lip to keep from asking. She couldn't ever recall seeing such an intense look on Paul's face, and the wet chill in the air certainly didn't help to lighten either of their moods.

After another good hour of driving, Paul pulled into the parking lot of a small, roadside diner. Having absolutely no idea where they were or how much farther they had to go, in an unconsciously cynical tone she asked him, "Is this just a pitstop, or are we meeting some mystery person here for lunch?"

His face tightened and immediately, Dierdre regretted having ever opened her mouth to breathe, let alone to speak. She was upset by the sudden look of hurt in his eyes.

"We have to talk," he answered, with his arms resting on the steering wheel and his hands folded in a prayer-like fashion.

"Why do I get the feeling this isn't going to be a pleasant surprise?" Dierdre muttered under her breath.

"What?"

"Nothing. I'm sorry. You were saying?" She didn't look at him, trying to swallow her fears.

"Let's go inside. I could really go for a cup of hot coffee. How about you, Sugar?"

"I don't want anything," she answered. "But you can."

"Come on, let's go in," he said.

The air was damp now and rain began to fall as he escorted Dierdre into the diner. Despite the tenseness of the moment, Dierdre was glad to be inside. The hot coffee Paul had ordered for her felt warm and comforting as it went down.

"You drank that pretty fast for someone who didn't want anything," he teased.

Without asking if she wanted more, he beckoned the waitress to refill Dierdre's cup along with his own and graciously thanked her for the speedy service. He reached for Dierdre's hand in a wordless effort to get her attention and said, "There's something I have to tell you." He began hesitantly staring into the cup. "Something I hope you don't hate me for, because I've hated myself about it for a very long time."

Dierdre looked at him with wide eyes. Her mind raced. Was this the part where he would admit to having a wife and kids, or being a felon, or something awful like that? Still silent, she looked up from her cup and caught his cloudy eyes. The lines of frustration and sorrow that became so familiar in recent weeks were edged even more deeply in his face. Seeing him this way frightened her. What secret could possibly be worse than her own had been? What tragedy more devastating that he could barely find the words to speak of it?

Unable to stand the silence between them any longer, she reached for his strong arms, and pulling them towards her across the table, she pleaded, "Paul, please tell me what's wrong. Whatever it is, we can work it out together."

"Oh, God, how do I explain this?" He searched the ceiling.

"Explain what, Paul? Where are we going? Where are we going that it's got you so upset? What is it, or who is it that you want me to see?"

"There's someone I need you to meet," Paul answered softly as he stared into his cup.

Tilting her head sideways, with hands still firmly clasped onto his forearms, Dierdre forced him to look at her. "Paul!" She was pressing him now, perhaps more than was wise of her, but the ghosts needed to be out of the closet. "What is it that is so difficult to tell me? Believe me, nothing you can reveal to me could be any worse than my revelations to you. Nothing you can tell me can be worse than what I've already experienced in my life." She spoke the words with steadfast conviction wrapped in desperate apprehension.

Chapter Twenty-Eight

P aul breathed a deep and woeful sigh. Shaking his head from side-to-side and staring deeply into Dierdre's eyes, with a heavy heart and words difficult to speak, he told her the truth about his past.

"I was married once," he said. "To a girl named Carolyn."

Dierdre instantly felt her jaw drop. Oh, God. He is married. Her mind raced, but she spoke not a word at this revelation.

"We met at a local bar through some mutual acquaintances, and after a couple of hours we were both pretty drunk. One thing led to another, and the next thing I knew, we were in the backseat of my car. I gave her some money for her trouble."

Oh, please, Dierdre thought, he can't mean the Mustang! And what's this about money?

"I went home that night not expecting to ever see or hear from her again, and I honestly didn't care to. I mean, she was hot and all, but it was just a one night thing. Or at least I thought so."

Dierdre listened intently, afraid of where this story might be going, but she tried to contain herself and remained silent.

"Anyway, about a month later, I was at the same tavern with some of my buddies, and the next thing I know she eyes me from across the room and then drags me into a corner. That's when she told me she was pregnant, and that she was certain I was the father. I didn't know whether to believe her or not. I sure didn't want to. I was twenty-one, and she was sixteen, but I didn't know how young she was at the time, honest I didn't! She looked and acted so much older than her age."

Dierdre's mind continued to race and pain filled her chest. She wanted to gasp for air, but all she could do was hold her breath.

"I must have asked Carolyn if she was sure a thousand times in a two-minute conversation, but she kept saying she was. And so I pleaded with her to have an abortion, rather than to give birth to a child that neither of us was ready for, but she wouldn't do it. She told her parents, and the next thing I know, I'm being threatened with rape charges. My entire future was going to hell if I didn't agree to marry her."

Dierdre still hadn't taken a breath.

"Four weeks later I was a married man, expecting a baby with a woman I barely knew, and didn't love. I was jobless and penniless, but I had a family on the way, and I had to do something. That's when I joined the Merchant Marine. I knew I could make a good living, and the idea of being away much of the time offered me the only sense of freedom I could find in all this mess I got myself into. Months at sea, no matter how difficult, had to be better than jail, which is where I was going if I didn't do things Carolyn's way. Whatever dreams I may have had before were gone now, and all because of one night of recklessness. I made a big mistake, and I had to pay for it with the rest of my life. I remember speaking a lot of lines on my wedding day. To love, and to honor this young girl that I slept with only once and wished I had never met. I felt a lot of anger for the child she was carrying, wishing every day that hatred alone was a powerful enough force to penetrate the womb that protected it and cause it to die. I despised myself for even thinking such awful thoughts, knowing full well that God would one day see fit to punish me, without mercy, for cursing this innocent child that I created."

Paul wasn't looking at Dierdre now, and she felt an odd relief in knowing that she didn't have to look into his eyes at this moment. She didn't know if she could do so without an expression of shock and disbelief. His story was beginning to have an all too familiar ring.

"The child was born while I was at sea. Carolyn sent a birth announcement, but not a photo, and so I knew nothing but the basics. It was a girl, weighing 7 lbs. 14 oz. at birth, and her name was Jessica Lynn. I had two more months of tour to get used to the idea of fatherhood, and to take real responsibility for bringing a life into the world that I knew would depend on me in so many ways. Part of me felt scared and cursed, but yet another part was curious. I wondered if she looked at all like me, and why I suddenly cared to know. But ready or not, I had a daughter, and I had a lot to learn."

Indeed he did, Dierdre thought.

"I arrived home and heard the baby cry as I pulled up the driveway of the small house we had been renting since the marriage. The cries grew louder as I stepped closer to the entrance and let myself in. I called to Carolyn. No answer. Without thinking, I dropped the gunnysack from my shoulders and walked closer to the bassinet in the living room. And there she was. I touched her little hands and toes. It surprised me how she seemed to like that, and her loud cries soon became a soft, pleasing whimper."

"So you're my kid? I asked as if expecting some sort of response from an infant. Before I realized it, I lifted her into my arms. She was cute as a button, and had an incredible likeness to me. I was actually surprised at how comfortable I felt holding her. After about ten minutes, Carolyn came out of the bedroom."

Dierdre continued to listen intently, trying desperately not to feel or show any emotion.

"Where were you, I asked her? The baby was crying."

"If you were home more you would know that it cries all the time. That's what babies do. They cry."

"I told her, well, I'm sorry if I'm not home all the time, but somebody has to pay the bills. This joke of a marriage wasn't my idea. If you recall, you insisted on having the kid, not me!"

"I was really annoyed now, and so I placed Jessica back in her bassinet. She started to cry again almost instantaneously."

"I never said I wanted a baby, Paul, she told me. It's all your fault. If I hadn't begged and pleaded with my parents, you'd be rotting in jail for the next fifteen years."

"Two minutes after I walked in the door and we were fighting like cats and dogs already. I told her, hey, you weren't so sweet and innocent when I met you. Your parents should know what you are. I just didn't have the heart to tell them that their precious daughter was a whore, that I had to pay for it like everyone else, and that you used the money to buy yourself any kind of fix you could get your hands on."

"She slapped me hard. She was popping again. Probably uppers. She always brought out the worst in me when she was high. I wondered how the baby was born healthy despite Carolyn's drug addiction. I wondered how I could have gotten myself into such a damned mess. Of all the guys she'd been with, and there were many, why was it me that got her pregnant? For the longest time I didn't believe that the child was really mine, but all thoughts about that were cast aside with my first glimpse of her just moments before. Jessica was my kid all right. She was the newborn of a ship-worn, young sailor for a father and a junkie and a whore for a mother. She was a beautiful baby, but I feared that my initial feelings were right. That Jesse would have been better off to never have been born than to be the product of two people who didn't even like each other, let alone love each other."

Dierdre couldn't help but notice that the tone in Paul's voice began to sound more desperate as he continued to tell his story. She allowed him to proceed without interruption.

"The next three months were a nightmare. Carolyn and I fought constantly. I knew she was resentful towards both me and the baby. She found every excuse imaginable to avoid spending time with either of us. And so, before I knew it, I took on the better part of our parental responsibilities, basically by default. By the time my next tour came due, I had really become quite attached to Jesse. I was saddened at the thought of having to leave her for three full months. And I was afraid. Carolyn's drug addiction was progressing at a steady pace. She was mixing pills with alcohol nearly every day and it scared me."

"The time pressed on, and by mid-December I was off again, leaving my young and fragile daughter in the care of a woman who could barely take care of herself. A year earlier, I would never have imagined the heartsick feeling that I felt during those last days at home. Even though marriage to Carolyn had grown less tolerable with each passing day, Jessica made it more bearable somehow. I hated to leave her. I wished that I could take her with me, and stow her away in a safe place where no one could find her, or do her harm. I wondered how I ever could have wished this child dead. I grew to love her so much in such a very short time."

Dierdre could clearly see the tears welling up in his eyes, but she still spoke not a word.

I left for tour one week before Christmas, but I decorated a huge tree and left a roomful of gift-wrapped presents for Jesse before heading off to my next port of call. I knew that she was too young to appreciate any of the effort, and would never recall my labors of love, but I had to do it, if not for my daughter, but for myself. I didn't know what else to do."

"Over the next two years Jesse grew from a beautiful infant to the most adorable little toddler on the planet. Somehow, despite my periods of absence, a bond developed between us. Meanwhile, Carolyn became a virtual stranger living under the same roof. She interacted with the baby and me only when necessary, and her drug addiction quickly become serious enough to leave her fitness as a mother in question. I suggested she seek professional help, but that only agitated her, and her parents proved unreceptive to any of my appeals. It was difficult for them, as parents, to accept the fact that their daughter was an addict, that she'd been sleeping around since a teenager, and that I was simply the poor slob who got caught up in a foolish mess. I got that. But the forced marriage and parental obligation served only to escalate her instability. She was like a timebomb waiting to explode, waiting to rupture with rage and resentment for the self-inflicted imprisonment that she saw fit to blame on her parents, her husband, her child, and anyone except herself. I shuddered at the thought that she might be on a path to suicide and that no one could stop her."

Dierdre searched deep inside herself to maintain some sense of composure as Paul's revelations cut forcefully into her own psyche. Part of her wished he would just stop talking, but if he could find the mettle to speak of it, she knew she had to find the courage to listen.

"I spent the last few weeks of my summer ship duty debating what few alternatives were available to me. I considered divorce, but feared the consequences to Jesse if my wife was given custody of the child, which would be the likely scenario unless I could unequivocally prove her unfit. I just couldn't take the chance of failure in that regard. Still,

I couldn't continue to chance the current situation either. I had to take some kind of action to ensure the safety and well-being of my child. That's when I decided to leave the Merchant Marine so I could be home permanently and better supervise Jessica's care. Somehow, I would figure out a way to support us. My daughter was all that mattered to me in the world. I couldn't wait to get home to her. She seemed to grow and change so much while I was away. Seeing her again at each tour's end made me heartsick over the lost time between us and the missed experiences of her childhood that was passing so quickly."

"My ship docked at homebase the weekend after Labor Day. Three years to this very day. It was well past midnight. While many of my friends chose to sleep on the ship until morning, I was eager to get home. I was giving notice of intent to resign at the end of the month. Soon, there would be no relief from the never-ending arguments with Carolyn. I hoped I could bear it. I prayed that loving Jesse as much as I did would be enough to ease the sting of what I knew was coming. Regardless, I had made my decision. I was staying home now, for good."

"I felt excited when the taxi pulled up in front of the house. I couldn't wait to get inside. Jesse would be sound asleep, but I decided that it would be okay to wake her. I knew she would be thrilled to see me. And then......" Paul cringed, and threw his face in his hands.

Instinctively, Dierdre reached out and took his hands in hers. She held them tightly, staring into his now red and tear-soaked eyes.

"And then I saw them. Carolyn's body strewn on the kitchen floor with pills of every shape, size, and color scattered beside her. And Jessica, just a few feet away. I touched my fingers to the baby's neck. She had no pulse. Frantic, I puffed air into her mouth, trying to resuscitate her, attempting to breathe life back into my precious baby. Please, God please! I begged. I thought, this can't be happening. How could you let this happen? I remember screaming those words at the body of my dead wife crumpled on the floor, but her soul was beyond the sound of my cries. If she wasn't already gone, I know I would have killed her. How could Carolyn and I have been so stupid? So careless? So selfish in the failures of our marriage, that we risked the life of our precious, innocent child?"

Dierdre and Paul were both trembling now, but their hands remained firmly entwined.

"And then, by the grace of God, I saw movement in Jesse's little chest. She blinked, and whimpering sounds suddenly gurgled up from her windpipe. My little angel stood on the edge of death, but she was clinging to life. She was alive! Thank the Lord, my baby was alive!"

Although trying desperately not to display shock at what she was hearing, Dierdre couldn't help but breathe a great sigh of relief. She continued gazing intently into Paul's blue eyes, desiring to know more. "So she's okay?"

Paul shook his head from side to side. "No, Dee, she's not okay."

"I don't understand. She survived."

"Yes, she survived. She returned from the shadows of death, but she was never the same. She went without oxygen for too long a time. Her brain was damaged beyond repair, and she can never live a normal life."

"Oh, my heavens!"

"And it was all my fault! I wished her dead at first. I wanted them to cut her up and throw her in the garbage so that I could be free. But then I grew to love her. I knew she wasn't safe, but I was too late."

"Paul, you did all you could do. You saved her life."

"Life? What life?" He cried softly as he buried his head in his hands once more. "She'll never be the same. She was a perfect baby and now she'll never be right. Life is precious, and fragile. A strong body and an able mind are gifts from God that my baby will never know."

"Does that make you love her less?" she asked. "Are you ashamed of her?"

"No! I love her more than anything. I'll just never understand why God punished an innocent child for the selfishness and stupidity of her parents."

"God would never bring suffering to a child in order to punish another. Never!" Dierdre spoke with conviction and understanding, all the while remembering how hurt she felt when her own mother disclosed that she was never wanted, and that she would have aborted her if she could have. Her heart broke for the pain and guilt Paul carried with him for so many years.

"I'll never know what really happened. I'll never know whether Carolyn gave the pills to the baby on purpose, or if Jesse swallowed them thinking they were candy. I cursed my wife for her drug dependence. I cursed myself for being away from home too often, and for failing as a father. I made the gravest of mistakes by leaving the care of my child in the hands of a woman I knew to be unstable and unfit. I should have known better. I have no excuses. It was my fault that my child became permanently disabled. I can never forgive myself."

"Just how impaired is she, Paul?" Dierdre asked tentatively, knowing that the question, no matter how delicately put, would burn him.

"She's bad. She can't talk, walk, or dress herself. She can't feed herself." His voice broke. "But she's beautiful. She's the prettiest kid in the world."

"So she looks like you? Dierdre smiled. Were you taking me to see her?"

He nodded.

"Yes, what? That she looks like you, or that were taking me to see her?"

"Both," he answered with a slight grin. "Do you want to meet her?"

"If you want me to."

Frustration and guilt remained etched into his reddened face. "Are you sure?"

Dierdre looked deeply into his eyes and said, "Paul, you are the kindest, most wonderful man I have ever known. I love you so much. And I know that in whatever way possible, Jesse loves you too. She is very lucky to have you as her father. We're only human, and we all make mistakes. You took responsibility when other men wouldn't. You didn't abandon your baby, or her mother. We can't turn back the clock or change the past, no matter how much we wish it were possible. And letting go is really hard. Nobody knows that better than me. Take me to see her, Paul. Yes. Take me to meet your daughter."

Chapter Twenty-Nine

They arrived at the Seasider Rehabilitation Center just before noon. The rain had tapered off, but a sky full of clouds continued to darken the day such that mid-afternoon seemed almost like approaching nightfall. The cobblestone roadway winded through the scenic grounds. Dierdre was in awe at the truly spectacular landscape that stretched for miles. The Tudor-style buildings were architecturally stunning with deep red and brown hues, and each had a view of the ocean that appeared from all angles to be just a stone's throw away. Even the grayness of the day couldn't camouflage the true splendor of this place that was nothing like the sterile, dreary, hospital-like facility that she had imagined. Seasider appeared more like a country club than an institution for the physically and emotionally challenged. As Paul pulled into the parking area, Dierdre was suddenly more aware of how expertly he maneuvered each curve of the road, each turn about the grounds. He was familiar with this place. He had come here often.

Paul led her from the car in silence. His trembling hand grasped hers firmly, and they entered the Visitor's Center arm-in-arm.

"Mr. Wellington, how good to see you again," the receptionist said, acknowledging his arrival with a handshake and a smile. She gazed in Dierdre's direction. "And your friend?"

"Oh, I'm sorry, Mrs. McKay. This is Dierdre."

Dierdre and Mrs. McKay shook hands cordially and exchanged smiles as Paul signed the guest log for both of them.

"You know where to go. Give Jesse a hug for me," she continued, as she closed the registry.

Paul and Dierdre stepped down the carpeted hallway and up the spiral staircase to the Day Room. Dierdre was impressed with the plush and appealing atmosphere. This must be costing him a fortune, she thought.

"Paul, this is truly spectacular! What a lovely place. I've never seen anything like it."

He smiled. "I searched a long time for this place," he answered. "I guess I knew I could never have her with me, but I thought if she was somewhere near the ocean at least I would feel like I was close to her all the time."

"You love her very much, don't you?"

"More than anything. Until you came along, Jesse was all I had."

Dierdre kissed him softly on the cheek. "Well, now you have two women who are crazy about you, Sailor. Think you can handle it?"

"I don't know, but I'm sure willing to try."

The door to the Day Room was open as they approached the end of the second floor hallway. Dierdre could barely believe her eyes. She saw children everywhere, of all different ages. Most sat in wheelchairs, and were very small and frail in appearance. Dierdre guessed that the room was occupied by twenty or so boys and girls. She recognized one or two with obvious cases of Down Syndrome and cerebral palsy, but most of the children looked entirely normal at a glance. However, upon closer observation, their various disabilities became more apparent. She observed that few were capable of discernible speech, and several appeared to suffer from sight impairments. Many of them also lacked normal motor coordination. Regardless of their afflictions, however, each and every one had the pure and unspoiled face of an angel.

Dierdre searched the room thoroughly as Paul stood silent and motionless at her side. "Which one is Jessica?"

She followed the direction of his eyes, and then she saw her. "Well, are you going to introduce me?"

Paul nodded. Holding her hand firmly in his, he led her across the room to meet his child. Jessica barely raised her head as they approached.

"Does she know that we're here?"

"Sometimes she's aware, but most of the time not," Paul whispered.

A face that had worn a pained grimace for the better part of the day now reflexively turned into a wide smile as he approached his daughter. Jessica was a beautiful child, with very blonde hair and bright blue eyes. Indeed, she held a truly remarkable resemblance to her father.

"Jesse, it's Daddy," Paul called, as his hand reached out to brush the golden locks from her cheeks in a gentle and caressing manner.

He turned back towards Dierdre. "I guess this isn't one of her better days. She's usually more responsive on a sunny day." The disappointment in Paul's eyes was unmistakable, their quickly having lost the glow that emanated from them just moments before.

"I'm sorry, Honey," Dierdre said, as she put her arm around his neck. "She's a very pretty little girl, Paul."

Tears filled his eyes again as he gazed upon his precious child.

"Paul, it wasn't your fault. You have to believe that."

"I can't believe that. I can't," he said with a trembling voice. "I let it happen. I knew something terrible was coming. I felt it in my gut, but I didn't act fast enough. She was perfect. Perfect. Now she's like this. She'll always be like this. Why has God used her to punish me?"

"Paul, God hasn't punished anyone. Look at all of these other children. Has God punished all of them, too? Or their parents? I can't explain why this has happened to Jesse, or to any of these kids. I've come to realize that there are a lot of things in this life that we can never understand. And even the pains of the past that we do eventually come to terms with never really go away. We just learn to accept them as a part of who we are now. We learn to go on. To make the present and the future better than the past in whatever way possible. You love Jesse and she loves you. And so do I. Nothing else matters."

Dierdre wrapped her arms around Paul's neck as Jessica lifted her head to look in their direction. "See, I told you she loves you. Jesse knows a really great guy when she sees one, right Jesse?"

Dierdre offered a warm and loving smile. "Forgive yourself, Paul.

You owe it to your daughter. You may never be able to bury the pain, but you have to bury the guilt."

"I swear, you are the best thing that ever happened to me. You and my daughter. I guess I stole the right set of car keys that last night of class after all."

They shared a mellow, but warm-hearted laugh that encouraged another vague, yet noticeable reaction from Jesse, whose angelic blue eyes remained fixed on them for the remainder of the afternoon.

Chapter Thirty

They left Seasider just as the sun was beginning to set on the horizon. The relief Paul felt was clearly evident in his softer, less pained visage.

"Sugar, you are rare jewel," he said, as they were once again driving down the winding cobblestone path. "You suffered so much of your own personal pain, and still you speak of understanding and forgiveness. Sometimes, I believe you're an angel sent from Heaven, come to save me. I will never let you go."

"I'm not going anywhere, Paul."

"I want you to marry me. I need you to marry me. Will you marry me?"

Dierdre's jaw dropped at the question, but without further hesitation she smiled widely and answered an exuberant, "Yes!"

Paul was on duty again from October through February, and they planned to be married the following spring. While they were apart the better part the winter holidays, a spiritual closeness that even time and distance couldn't change existed between them. Dierdre's visits to Seasider were frequent during these months before the wedding. She was quite familiar to Jessica now, and the child responded with ever-so-subtle movements of her head and hands to the touch and smell of her.

Her love for this child and for Paul brought out the best in Dierdre. Many an afternoon she sat with Jesse in the Day Room and spent countless hours reciting the ever-growing volume of poems and stories she was inspired to write. What a wonderful stimulus love could be, she thought. What a joyous way to express one's affection for others, for oneself, and for all things in life. She was very fortunate, and happier than she had ever believed possible.

Was it possible for life to change so much? Was it conceivable to turn a life that had been so preoccupied with shame, distrust and bitterness into one filled with an overabundance of joy and peace? Could the love of one man open a heart that had been sealed so tightly for so long?

More and more, Dierdre realized that just as Paul had breathed the life back into his child years ago, so too had he breathed life into her. He was magic, and both she and Jessica were the living products of his very special kind of love.

Paul returned home in mid-March. Dierdre planned a small wedding ceremony and reception for the first of May. To Paul's surprise, she made special arrangements for Jesse to attend with the help of a pediatric nurse. They intended to move to the suburbs. The pending relocation forced Dierdre to resign her position at the publishing company. In a few short years she had been promoted from an entry-level proofreader to an editor. She even managed to have a few of her own poems and short stories published with the help of some friends in the company. Dierdre felt ready, however, to make writing a full-time occupation. She also wanted to be closer to Jesse at Seasider. They needed to be a real family now, to build a life based on the trust, hope, and love that had brought them together in the first place. Jessica's care was expensive, and so it wasn't prudent for Paul to consider leaving the Merchant Marine as he had in the past. Despite the fact that he was gone full-time for so many months out of the year, the time that he was home was very special.

Dierdre grew accustomed to Paul's periods of absence. With the new home, and a daughter, as well as her writing to keep her busy, loneliness and depression were a thing of the past. She recalled that for the first twenty years of her life, "family," had been a dirty word, one associated with deceit, insincerity, pain and selfishness. A word that stood for nothing good and everything bad. Her union with Paul redefined the word, "family," such that it was now synonymous with love, warmth, and happiness, and all of the good and blessed things in life. No more holding back for fear of rejection. No more physical or emotional abuse. No more cursing the God who brought two once very lonely and heartsick people together. Who gave both she and Paul the strength to confront the fears deep in their hearts, and the courage to share them with each other. Who turned souls once frozen in the sorrows of the past, into spirits moving freely forward into the joys of both the present and the future.

The marriage of Paul and Dierdre proved to be a truly joyous occasion. All of the tenants from the brownstone were there. Mr. D. gave the bride away. Marion was Maid of Honor, and Jay, a long-time, mariner friend of Paul's was the Best Man. Dierdre's invitation to her mother was graciously declined. Despite all that had happened in the past, Dierdre hoped she would attend, but she accepted that they would never know the closeness of other mothers and daughters, and tried not to let her absence ruin her special day.

Dierdre and Paul made a beautiful couple on their wedding day, she in her flowing, white gown, and he also dressed in white to match. Perhaps the most precious sight, however, was Jessica. Dressed in pink from head to toe, she looked like a cherub as she sat beside them at the altar. Speechless and near motionless in her wheelchair, the look of a smiling child glowed from deep inside of her. They were a family now, in a newly defined sense of the word, and life was all good.

Chapter Thirty-One

The following two years flew by. Dierdre's writing talents flourished during this period in which she won reasonable acclaim for two books of poetry and several short stories. Her work grew steadily in popularity and the critics were, for the most part, kind. Paul was also doing well. He gained considerable status since their marriage, which served to increase his salary as well as his perks. Without question, the marriage had proven good for both of them.

Jessica's condition remained unchanged. Dierdre and Paul loved her dearly and prayed that, in whatever way possible, Jesse could understand how much she meant to them. Many a summer's evening, they sailed the Folly up the coast past the splendor of Seasider, waving their arms in the sunset as they passed the Day Room window where Jessica sat each day. They shared their love of the sea with her in this way, and were grateful for the once-elusive peace of mind they had discovered there together. Deep in their souls, Jesse was always with them. In their minds she could smell the salty air and feel the sun beating warmly against her face. She could hoist a sail and catch and clean a fish. She could laugh, and she could smile, and she could live the carefree life of a child.

"Paul, we've really been very lucky these past few years," Dierdre murmured in bed in a half-state of sleep, exhausted from a busy weekend on the boat.

"We sure are," he answered, rolling over with a heavy sigh.

"Really, Paul," she said, leaning on her side to face him, and propping her head up against his shoulder. "Sometimes I feel almost guilty that we're so happy. Maybe we should start going to church or something. To express our gratitude."

His tightly closed eyelids flew open. He encircled her in his arms, kissing her repeatedly in a lighthearted fashion. "Can we be grateful tomorrow, Sugar? This dude's had a rough day and needs some sleep."

"You think I'm being silly, don't you?"

"No, you're not being silly, but your timing is really bad. Can we talk about this tomorrow? I'm really beat."

"Tomorrow? Paul, what if we didn't have tomorrow? What if something happened and today was our last tomorrow?"

"You're acting weird now, Honey."

With his shoulders resting against the headboard and his arms folded over his chest, Paul sat up. "Okay. What's the matter? You're beginning to sound very paranoid."

"Nothing is the matter. That's the point. Everything is wonderful. Our marriage is terrific. Our daughter is beautiful. Our lives are nearly perfect," Dierdre responded.

"So what's the problem? It isn't like we haven't both had our share of hard times, you know. We both paid a lot of dues. We deserve to be happy. Everyone does."

"Oh, I know that. I know, and I'm not complaining. It's just that I'm scared."

"Scared of what?"

"I really don't know. Maybe you're right. Maybe I'm just being paranoid. It's just that I've never had anything to lose before. Not until now. My life has never been so delightful. Sometimes I think I must be dreaming and that one day I'll wake up to discover that all of the good things will never have been real."

"But it is real, Sugar. Touch me. I'm real." He grasped her hands firmly. "Now come on over here, cuddle with your favorite sailor, and forget about it, okay? Everything is fine. Nothing bad is going to happen. We're going to live in a state of marital bliss until death do us part and all that mushy stuff."

Slowly, he moved her closer. His nearness always made her feel safe and secure. She was so lucky to have found him. As she watched her husband fall back to sleep beside her, Dierdre recalled the sense of comfort she had once found in being alone, and being accountable to no one but herself. She was glad those days were over. Her life was so much fuller now, more so than she had ever dreamed possible. She was grateful to accept the blessings of the present and could only pray that the future would bring more of the same.

Chapter Thirty-Two

Paul was scheduled for a late summer tour of duty that year and soon he would be off again for the next several months. The previous spring was busy, and much of their time was spent in renovating their home and in training the black Labrador retriever puppy Paul brought home as a surprise for their second wedding anniversary. Sentiment dictated, of course, that he be named Max. From the very first day, the pup followed Dierdre everywhere. She fell in love with him instantly, and seemed to have great patience and a natural maternal instinct with the little guy. Dierdre and Paul had talked about having children of their own, but neither felt the timing was right just yet. And so the arrival of Max served to at least temporarily fulfill their desire for the pitter-patter of little feet in their home, even if they weren't human and came in a set of four instead of two.

Soon, those four little paws became very large ones, and Max grew into a strong and solid eighty-five pounds of dog. Paul and Dierdre took him everywhere and, as a result, Max soon became quite popular with all of the neighborhood and boatyard children. He became a powerful and steady swimmer, and was a frequent companion with them on the Folly. Somehow, they even managed to sneak him into Seasider to visit with Jesse, despite very strict regulations against such things.

Yes, after four wonderful months, Dierdre soon found herself once again waving farewell to her husband from the pier. She believed she would miss him more than usual this time, but couldn't understand why. Perhaps it was the time of year, or her growing desire to become a mother. She didn't know. All she knew was that the sadness in her heart upon his departure was very real, more so than ever before, and it frightened her.

With Max faithfully at her side, Dierdre proceeded slowly off the pier as she watched Paul's ship become ever smaller against the vast blue ocean that would again carry her husband far away.

"Daddy will be home soon," she said, in an attempt to assure both Max and herself. Her mournful and unsteady voice made the words come out sounding more like a question than a statement.

The house always seemed very large and exceptionally quiet when Paul was away, and particularly on his departure days. Max spent nearly every moment at Dierdre's side. That evening, he cuddled close to her with his heavy black head and muzzle resting over her shoulder as she struggled to fall asleep. I'll feel better tomorrow, Dierdre told herself over and over again praying that sleep would fall upon her and, as always, for God to watch over her husband while he was away.

She still felt depressed when she woke the next morning. As she took the last sip of her third cup of coffee, she could feel the buzz from having ingested too much caffeine. After several more hours of wandering around the house looking for things to do, Dierdre came to the realization that she would go absolutely insane over the next four months without engaging herself in a major project that would help pass the time. She pulled out her notebook for the first time in many months, laid it on the kitchen table, and then stared at it for a very long time. She had contemplated writing a novel in the past, but could never seem to find the courage to begin. She thought long and hard as she proceeded to pour herself a fourth cup of coffee. I suppose now is as good a time as ever, she told herself. What have I got to lose? With that thought, she grabbed a pen from the junk drawer and started to scribble down an outline for the book she always dreamed of writing.

Her efforts expressed unprecedented intensity from that day forward. She splurged on a computer and then, for the next three months, Dierdre wrote day and night. Her anticipation grew with the completion of each page, each chapter. On the days when words came easily, she would often sit for hours mesmerized by the fantasy world she created with each stroke. She missed her husband terribly, but the days seem to pass more quickly when she was writing. The mental exhaustion she often experienced after a long day made sleep come easier at night. She was determined to complete the first draft before Paul returned home for Thanksgiving. She wanted so much for this to be the best work she had ever done. She wanted Paul to be proud of the accomplishment, prouder of her than he had ever been. Paul had changed her life so much. He gave her life when she had nearly given up. He taught her how to love, how to give and forgive, and how to find pleasure in the simple things. He taught her the meaning of faith and trust, in others as well as in herself, and to believe that anything was possible, that dreams could become reality. But more than anything, he helped her to recognize that she deserved to be happy. Yes, she was truly blessed. By transforming a once bitter heart into one warm with understanding and love, Paul offered her a new and wonderful beginning.

By late October, her book was nearly complete and Dierdre found herself anxious for Paul to return home. She couldn't wait for him to read it. As insecure as she often was about her work, she felt good about this most recent endeavor. Paul's approval was of great importance to her, however. In many ways, she thought of her writing as a team effort since so much of her inspiration came from him. She hoped he would be pleased. His ship was due back to port very soon and, as always, she would be waiting at the pier to take him home.

She wanted and needed him now more than ever and yes, she was ready to have his child as well. Dierdre hoped that, with any luck, by this time next year her book would be published and a new life would be created. These two labors of love would be living and lasting testaments to their union that would remain long after she and Paul were gone from this earth. They would be mortals made immortal by these creations, one of flesh-and-bone and the other of the intangible, but ever-so-powerful written word.

Fate had been kind, and Dierdre felt selfish in asking for more than those blessings that had already been bestowed upon her. Yet, she chose to have faith in the words of her husband. To believe that she should accept the good as easily as the bad, ask no questions, and understand that everything would always happen for the best. She would try to do just that, for it was her unfailing trust in Paul that had brought her a true happiness that, previous to their meeting, had only existed in her dreams.

Chapter Thirty-Three

Dierdre lay wide awake in bed. She looked at the alarm clock on the nightstand. 3 a.m., and she still hadn't slept a wink. Paul was due back on the eighteenth of November, and as that day drew nearer, she found it increasingly more difficult to sleep. It would be light in a few hours, she thought.

Fluffing the pillows and rearranging the bed covers, she turned over on her side in a seemingly futile effort to fall back to sleep. As Dierdre lay motionless in bed, with Max resting comfortably at her feet, she could both feel and hear the pounding of her heart deep within her chest. The beats were hard and heavy, and the eerie silence of the night served only to encourage an odd sense of uneasiness within her. Soon, she gave up entirely on the notion of slumber and found herself sitting on the edge of the bed and staring out the bedroom window.

Mother Nature had sent the first snows early on this eleventh of November, and although winter was officially still many weeks away, the cold chilled her bones. As Dierdre gazed wide-eyed into the blankets of white that covered the streets below, her legs tucked tightly beneath her, her mind raced with thoughts and emotions. Never before had she felt so anxious about Paul's return. She wished so much that he was there with her at that very moment so that she could hold him close and keep them safe from the frigidness of the outside air. She longed to make a baby and, in doing so, ensure the immortality of the love they shared. Soon, Dierdre was lost in imagining what a child of their union would look like. As her mind envisioned the babe as a smaller version of Jessica, the ringing of the doorbell suddenly startled her back to reality.

Who could be coming to call at this ungodly hour?

Quickly, she threw on a robe and ran down the stairs towards the front door, recalling the morning years ago when Paul had surprised her with an earlier than scheduled return home. Exhilarated, she opened the door.

"Jay, it's you. Hi."

"Hi, Dierdre," Jay responded, bending his head down low so that his deep brown eyes stared at his feet below.

"Jay, what is it?" Her heart began to pound so intensely that she believed it would burst from her chest. "Jay, what is it? What happened? Where is Paul? Is he okay?"

"There's been an accident," Jay replied, as he looked tearfully into her eyes.

"An accident? What kind of accident? Where is Paul, Jay?" She began to cry uncontrollably. "Jay, please! What happened to him? Is he hurt? Where is he? Where is my husband?"

"He's gone, Dierdre. He's gone." Jay spoke the words with a solemnness that she had never heard in his voice before.

"He's what?"

"He's dead. I'm so sorry."

Jay was crying now as Dierdre felt her knees buckle beneath her. She held on tightly to the door to keep from falling down.

"We rushed him to the hospital as fast as we could, but it was too late. He was gone before we got there. They tried to resuscitate him, but there was nothing they could do."

Dierdre believed her heart had stopped beating. She told herself over and over again that this was simply a bad dream, that she would soon awake and that everything would be alright. Paul would be coming home next Sunday and she would meet him at the pier just as she always did. They would make love and make a baby. They would share the holidays together with Jesse. They would once again sail the Folly beyond the sunset on a warm, summer's day and experience their own special Heaven on earth created from the love, trust, and devotion that flourished between them.

Dierdre didn't remember much that followed in the next several hours, only bits and pieces of conversations. She recalled something about the taxi he was riding in having been in an accident on the way home, that Jay was with him and was spared any injuries, that Paul took the brunt of the impact when the vehicle skidded into a guardrail. She recalled something about claiming his body at the morgue and making funeral arrangements. Most of the events of that dreadful Sunday, the eleventh of November, were destined to remain vague and distant in her memory. Anything was easier than acknowledging in her mind that which her heart simply couldn't bear to accept.

Chapter Thirty-Four

Paul was buried three days later. He was eulogized and laid to rest in the finest and most honorary fashion, but Dierdre responded little to words spoken during the lengthy ceremonies.

When she returned home alone on the afternoon of his interment, reality finally began to sink in. Her beloved husband was gone from this life, from her life. She wouldn't be picking him up at the pier next Sunday. She was alone again. Desperate and afraid just as she had been when she first ran away from home so many years ago. For many nights, she cried herself to sleep, and for many mornings thereafter a sick feeling in her stomach prevailed. The snow-covered earth served now only as a bitter reminder of her grief. All she could do was believe that Paul's spirit was somewhere safe and warm, knowing full well that his stiff and lifeless body rested beneath a blanket of ice in the cold, hard ground.

A few days later, she forced herself to look through Paul's belongings. His satchel was filled with dirty laundry. Reflexively, she began separating the whites from the colors, recalling that glorious day many years ago when she evolved from a child into a woman. She held tightly to each item pulled from the bag, smelling every one, wanting to hold on to whatever she could of the man she loved. As she reached into the bottom, she felt something hard and square. Extending her arm further down to grasp it more firmly, she pulled out the article that was wrapped carefully amidst the clothing. Drawing it to her breast, she wept until dawn.

On Christmas Eve, Dierdre finally found the strength to visit Jesse at Seasider. Along the way, she stopped to lay a small wreath of holly and evergreen on her husband's grave. Her eyes were still red and swollen from crying when she met Jessica in the Day Room, but she made every effort to conceal her sorrow as best she could. Despite her efforts, however, the child seemed sensitive to her somber mood and leaned her head on Dierdre's trembling shoulder. Dierdre tried to explain about Paul's death, and how it was just the two of them now. She assured Jesse that her father loved her very much, and prayed that somehow his beloved child could understand that he had not abandoned them. That he was a good man, that God had taken him to Heaven, and that they would see him again one day.

Dierdre remained at Seasider for the better part of that afternoon, most of which she spent in the silent, but loving arms of the beautiful child Paul had left in her care. She had to find the strength to go on, for Jesse and herself. Each other was all they had now, each other and the warm and tender memories of a man who, through his great capacity for love, had given them both the precious breaths of life.

Just as the sun was beginning to set, she reached into her purse, drawing from it the journal found amidst Paul's laundry. Bringing it to her quivering mouth, she kissed the cover, whose gold embossed imprint read, *The Sea of Dreams. A Sailor's Life, by Paul Wellington.*

As she gazed out the Day Room window to the ocean below, she couldn't help believing that Paul was out there somewhere. He so loved the sea. The serenity and peace of mind he discovered there was as much a part of him as the precious child sitting beside her. Yes, Paul belonged to a bigger world now, a better universe, where nothing hurt, and where tranquility and love existed among all God's creatures. He was a part of all things, of the sun and the sky above, the moon and the stars, the earth and the sea from which all life had evolved. Paul would live always in her heart, in their share dreams, and the realities yet to be fulfilled.

Dierdre read quietly aloud from Paul's private journal. This wonderful gift that he left behind, which bore his soul, and the very essence of his being, was all that she and Jesse had left of him. She prayed it would be enough to survive the rest of their lives without him.

When Dierdre returned home that night, Max greeted her with his usual tail-wagging exuberance. With a brisk pat on Max's head, and a rapid gait, Dierdre rushed to the kitchen and lifted the draft of her novel that lay on the table. In a sweeping motion, she thumbed through the numerous pages. Realizing there was now an entirely different and more important story to tell, without a second glance, she tossed the entire manuscript into the trash can beside her, pulled up a chair, and pulled out a clean piece of paper.

Chapter One, Page One. She typed with one very purposeful finger, and a mind and heart surging with the determination and courage of one-hundred men.

Epilogue

Dierdre took a long, deep breath as she lifted her eyes from the last page of the book. The flowery skirt she wore swirled fiercely in the breeze. The wind had picked up significantly, and the chill in the air became a bitter cold one in the few short hours since she began reading on the deck of the Folly. The once bright lights of the city in the foreground were dimmed now such that only the glow of the moon and stars remained to brighten the evening sky. Clutching the text in one hand and a glass of chardonnay in the other, she slowly walked the perimeter of the boat. Stopping to marvel at the pink and blue sails as they danced in the wind, she turned to one of the unnumbered pages in the front of the book and absorbed the few short sentences written there in silence. Raising the wine to her lips, she stared up at the stars, lifted the glass as if to toast the heavens, and swallowed the few drops that remained. With one final glance at the night sky, Dierdre lay the book open-faced on the deck. Carefully, she placed her now empty glass atop the page she had just finished reading and, with a heavy sigh, bid goodnight to the sea and began the long journey home. As the evening breeze continued to sing, the glass trembled over the edges of the delicate, wind-curled manuscript page whose words came truly from the heart. The dedication read:

To my dearest Paul. Husband, lover and friend. Together we learned the meaning of love and the importance of forgiveness. You filled my spirit with enough joy, courage and inspiration to last one-hundred lifetimes. Always shall I remember you. Always shall I hear your voice in the whistling of the wind that celebrates the joys of life and love and sings for all eternity *Beyond the Sea of Dreams.*